"Dear Noah the World"

by

Maggie Reid

reidmaggie@aol.com

i

We are all on a journey. Sometimes we are helped... sometimes we are hindered ...

Sometimes we don't know the way. The journey makes no sense to us, but it is ours. It is ours.

Dear Noah.... the World

Prologue

"How long have you been sitting in the darkness, Jessie?"

"I like the dark. I don't have to think. I don't have to do anything but imagine there is a blanket around me and I'm safe."

The briefcase clicked open. "You have thought about everything we talked about? I think I made all the criteria very clear to you regarding Noah. If you take a look at number three, next to the asterisk we ask that you make no visible contact with Noah... (in his best interests)."

I could feel my heart pounding. I was numb. Noah was sitting on the floor colouring a picture. I was grateful he was oblivious to what I had signed.

"The fostering of Noah is a temporary measure, and we ask that in any difficulty you contact the telephone numbers provided, until your psychiatric visit..."

"You think I am a bad mother don't you? You hate me. You gave me no option, it was fostering or blank, fostering or nothing. I hate you. I really do.

You think because I'm young I am stupid. I have no feelings. Look at Noah's coat. It's the best. I used every bit of money I got on that coat, and his shoes. It's important to have the right shoes when you are small. It's important... I know that. If I was a bad mother I would not know that, would I?"

"It would be best if you collect Noah's overnight bag, his schoolbag, and any toys he is used to... If you collect them now Jessie, that would be best..."

"I... I... I... have changed my mind... <u>Don't</u> take my little boy away from me... he's all I've got... no... no... no... don't take him... please... no..."

"Jessie, I need Noah's coat and bags please... nice and calm please, Jessie..."

"No... I won't... I won't give you his bags... This is the start... You won't bring him back... I read him books... I do... I... I... have his numbers all on little cards..."

It was a blur. Noah's coat was put on him by what was a stranger. I could not look at Noah. My frozen fingers were welded to the fragmented window sill.

I was sobbing. I could not see.

"Mummy... Mummy..." I could hear the words but I was frozen to the spot that was my refuge. My toenails felt pain. My eyes were closed.

"Wave to Mummy, Noah."

I could not look. I could not turn around, because it was never something I wanted to do.

I knew they were wrong. They had me so wrong.

Noah was still screaming as he was lifted into the car, tears streaming down my face, as his.

The car was an awful murky blue. Desperate, I ran downstairs leaving my front door wide open.

I was too late... the car sped away, and I sat on the pavement holding Noah's spare coat, just in case it rained. I held on to the wrought iron railings, screaming until the torrential rain exhausted me.

I would never forget that day.

Betrayal and being judged would become my reason for everything I would do, land every decision that I would make.

I had a backbone of steel, and for Noah I would make my fortune.

Chapter One

"Your name?" The elderly woman clad in a berry velvet tunic and oversized amber pendant looked sullen.

I didn't want to give my name. I wanted anonymity.

"My real name?"

The woman seemed to lose patience and tapped her foot three times.

"Look lovie, I don't care who you really are, or where you have come from. You can cartwheel on a zip-wire in a circus for all I care. My name is Bridget, and I don't ask questions. I need a name for the clients, different from your own. You are responsible for your own taxes."

I gulped. "You been in trouble with the law, Missy?"

I was astonished she would ask such a question. I almost felt hurt, but my feet were sore from walking.

"No... Miss... I haven't... I don't have an up to date passport... but I can get one... I <u>really</u> need this job."

Bridget poured me a cup of tea, and the crockery looked like real china, very expensive.

"I take what I do very seriously. I am fourth generation Romany, and I know what it is to always have to move on. I know what it is to be told to leave shops because they didn't want my "dirty money". I might have been married at eighteen, but I ain't no fool. If there is any trouble... I mean a client you don't want to read for, there is a panic button underneath the table. There is also a safety password... ghetto, if there is someone you don't like the look of.

You'll get to know the police. They always have fancy watches, and their eyes dart around the room like magpies, looking for evidence.

You see, they think Psychics rob folk blind... what they don't see is that none of my Psychics drag clients upstairs kicking and screaming. You'll see most of the fold we get here want someone to talk to... they are You see, they think Psychics rob folk blind... what they don't see is that none of my Psychics drag clients upstairs kicking and screaming. You'll see most of the folk we get here want someone to talk to... they are lonely. Yes, they might ask about love, relationships, and if they are going to win the lottery, but mostly they need an ear. You get me?

I don't read, or write, or have any fancy education but I know what's right and wrong, and I think in my own small way I help people.

You done Psychic work before?"

I hadn't, but didn't want to say. I shrugged my shoulders, and was too afraid to sip my tea.

"What's in your bag, missy. We don't do drugs here... if you are caught, it's instant dismissal. No drinking either, mind. You need your mind clear. So... what's in your bag"

I stared at the bottom of the teacup.

"Everything, all I have is in the bag..."

Bridget reached out her hand. "Your husband kicked you out like a stray cat to fend for yourself, eh? Long time ago... I thought there were fairytales, now I know there are no knights, there is only plain hard graft.

Do you have money in your pocket?"

I think she already knew the answer, so I told the truth.

"Not right now, but I've got my Nan's ring... After this I'm going to the pawn shop."

Bridget reached into the pocket of her tunic and pulled out notes.

"A friend of Bridget is a friend for life, take it..."

I knew I couldn't take charity. I knew it simply wasn't possible.

"Thank you, but I can do this job, I know I can..."

Bridge smiled. "You don't need an interview. You are one of the rare ones. You shine like a diamond. You are a channeller. You saw things as a child, didn't you... but were afraid to tell. You don't need even a set of tarot cards, because you don't need them. They would only be a prop.

You will get paid weekly in cash and you are paid by the reading, so it makes sense to treat the folks that come in here like kings and queens. You must <u>never</u> say where you come from, your date of birth, or reveal anything that could be used against you. You cannot talk about health or babies, and the rest is up to you."

I suddenly felt elated, there was a glimmer of hope.

"Do you mean I have the job. I didn't tell you my name..."

Bridget laughed... a gravely sort of laugh that I am sure could strip paint.

"Your name is <u>Almodine</u>, that's all you need to know..."

Chapter Two

It had been a strange morning. I couldn't believe Bridget knew nothing about me, and didn't even know my name, but she had given me enough money to eat for the next few weeks.

I promised that I would meet Matty who just appeared in my life, well maybe not so much appeared as such, but he introduced me to oysters and I was as sick as a dog for three days afterwards.

Matty and I eat in "Delaney's" which only people in the know can find. Located down a dimly lit cobbled street, with curved windows adorned with twig trees.

"Delaney's" has curved tables that mould themselves to the uneven stone floors like pieces of a jigsaw. The specials board seems to get bigger by the day, and there is never any shortage of optimism.

The owner is Aoife Delaney. I couldn't pronounce her name at first but Matty laughed raucously as he told me that Aoife just cared about turning a coin, not the way her name always seemed to be pronounced like spaghetti.

Aoife smiled at me with the largest animated smile that could light a Christmas tree.

"Matty is in the corner with enough rum to sink a pirate ship..."

Matty looked worse for wear.

"I need a cigarette..." Matty always needed a cigarette.

"How did the interview go? Did you get it?"

I felt a fool, especially as the interview lacked substance.

"I got it. I start tomorrow... just hope people want readings..."

Matty slugged his rum: "while the world turns... people want answers and you, my girl, will give them those answers... My old apartment may be yours today, tomorrow a castle. It's your chance."

Matty had known Bridget for years... funny, he had never thought to ask why...

Aoife brought the specials board. She read out the specials in her Irish accent that I think was a mixture of being in Cork, Dublin and New York.

"We have French onion soup; cream of onion soup; bangers, mash, onion gravy; and liver, bacon and onions."

Matty rolled his eyes playfully: "For goodness sake... did a few crates of onions fall off the back of a lorry?"

Aoife laughed: "You tease... Is it liver and onions, Matty?"

"Yep... as usual..."

"... and yourself... what can I get you?"

I didn't feel hungry, not at all. I suddenly felt cold, very, very, cold... chilled to the bone. I had no home to go to. I couldn't really tell anyone how I felt, but the pain felt like bricks being thrown at my feet till they bled.

"I have to go to see what I'm entitled to... you know..."

Aoife nodded. "The people that really need it the most never seem to be helped..."

Matty put his arm around me. "Come on, liver and onions is the cure for everything. Even those who want to destroy every bit of hope you have left..."

It was the biggest plate of liver, bacon and onions I had ever seen... I was forty years old, no home, and my child taken away. The rope bridge I felt I was crouching on was swinging from side to side.

Matty stayed in Delaney's while I attended my appointment with a thin woman with a face like old leather, and thin lips. My grandfather told me never to trust anyone with thin lips.

"My name is Deborah-Elise. I am here to assess what help, if any, you are entitled to. Fill in that form, sign it. I need proof of your previous earnings with bank statements... your child... reason he was taken from you?"

I felt like a clock face that had stopped.

"I... I... went... through a bad time."

Deborah-Elise tapped her chewed biro pen impatiently.

"Reason for your child being taken away...?"

I stuttered. There were people behind me waiting. "Nervous breakdown..." I whispered.

The woman seemed to grin in front of me. "If you had a <u>nervous</u> breakdown like you <u>say</u> you did, I'll need proof... <u>written</u> proof from a Doctor. You could be making it up for all I know..."

Deborah-Elise had said it so loud I felt a tear drip down my cheek.

"An assessor will be in touch..."

"What about my rent to be paid...?" I whispered.

"An assessor will be in touch in due course... Thank you..."

I stood up, wiping my face to remain dignified.

I walked slowly to Delaney's... and thought that I should try to call my little boy... the phone rang... and rang... and my ex answered abruptly.

"He is eating his dinner right now... not a good time... try later..."

At least my son would have all the material things at his father's that I could never give him.

I sat on a park bench, and tore up a paper napkin from "Delaney's" into a snowflake.

An elderly woman appeared in front of me. "Snowflakes still fall even when the sky is grey... they do you know..." She walked away...

I had sat on the park bench so long without my coat, because I wanted to feel the blood in my veins go cold. Hours bluer when your face is a clock face.

Chapter Three

Matty jangled the keys excitedly.

"This is my old apartment, it's been rented out a few times... it's compact and it's eh... well..."

Matty struggled to open the scratched front door that was painted an unfortunate shade of beige. The door knocker was hanging off.

Matty's face was aghast.

"Wow... they have taken everything. They have lifted carpets... the lot... even the light shades..."

The apartment looked bleak, cold and bleak. It was open plan which showed the fact that some of the kitchen cabinets had been ripped out in a hurry. There was no curtain on the huge sash window.

The smell was of cat urine, and cheap cologne.

I stayed calm. I was too tired other than to remain logical. "Is there a homeless shelter around here, Matty?"

Matty shook his head. "Not for miles I think... and even then, it's... you know..."

I nodded.

"You have to fulfil the criteria..."

I smiled, the biggest smile I could muster. An award winning Oscar performance.

"You know what, Matty... I think it's good... an empty shell... I could... you know... do something creative... I... I... love it..."

Matty looked agitated. "I had no idea... I... I... I should have checked... you could come to my parents'..."

Matty still lived with his parents. Matty had more money than most, and investments that he inherited. I had met Matty in a café, and he told me I was the most interesting person he had ever met...

"You go on, Matty... I've got my first day at Bridget's tomorrow. I am good, really..."

Matty bowed his head. "I should clean the place.... I should..."

"Matty, you have helped me with a roof over my head... I'm good... I really am..."

Matty left silently. I walked slowly to the one bedroom. There was a filthy, stained mattress on the floor. Bird droppings were beneath the window sill.

I was grateful to have the mattress. I didn't even light a candle. I just slept.

I woke with a start. I had time to grab a coffee at Delaney's and then a short walk to Bridget's.

I wore my grandmother's topaz ring. I needed all the help I could get today.

There was no mirror, and the sink was too filthy to wash. I sprayed myself with perfume and splashed my face with the coldest, iciest water.

I was ready. I twirled the topaz on my ring. I quickly braided my long, raven hair to give me anonymity, and remembered Bridget's words that I could say absolutely nothing about my life.

As I walked to Delaney's I tried to imagine who "Almodine" would be... Almodine was everything I wasn't. She was strong, successful, inspiring. She was honest. As Almodine I could never be hurt, or never disappointed.

Delaney's was quiet. The lights were dimmed.

I took out my pocket notebook. Each day when I would sit in Delaney's I would write as Almodine, so I would understand her whole history. I would know what would make her tick.

I wouldn't tell Matty, or anyone else. Almodine was my secret.

Chapter Four

Bridget stood at a polished desk smoking a cigarette.

"Your desk, Almodine. I have placed a crystal ball for effect. Readings are twenty minutes, unless you are told otherwise. A blue light at the side of the desk lights up when the full twenty minutes is over.

There is someone I want you to meet. This is Tristan. He does all the credit card bookings. I am glad you are early. You two can have a chat before your day begins.

Oh, and Almodine, remember password if you are in trouble, "ghetto". Oh... and one more thing... prepare for the unexpected."

Tristan looked elderly... and weak on his feet... but he had the most amazing, kind, ice blue eyes.

"Let me shake your hand young lady... it's Tristan... here to look after you."

I smiled. I needed someone to look after me.

"Don't worry... the first day is always the most difficult. Some people... they will try to catch you out, ask you for concrete evidence, and they will lash out if they don't get the right answers. Don't worry about these people.

Most of the people here... don't tell Bridget this... well... they are desperate. They have a mother who needs care, or they are church mice struggling to survive.

This is family here... we look after each other... we have to... the gypsies, the dreamers, those who believe in something else... we are always running."

Chapter Five

I sat at the desk. I couldn't help but fidget. My whole body was shaking uncontrollably.

Tristan smiled at me: "I didn't ask your real name Almodine... a gentleman always asks a lady's name..."

I could tell Tristan was a good person. His eyes... his calmness.

"My name is Jessie... and just to let you know... your wife... she is always with you... she says she is with Nanette..."

Tristan looked aghast. "I knew you were genuine, Jessie. Nanette is my mother, and I started working with Bridget... just taking the credit cards when my wife... when she..."

Tristan's eyes were glazed, but I could see the intense love that they had.

"You have made my day, young lady. Everyone does this job for a reason... you don't need to tell me..."

I took a deep breath. "I want... I _need_ to get a nice house... a _good_ place... I... want to get my little boy back... I _need_ that..."

"You are just a kid... What age were you when you had your son?"

"I was sixteen... he was older... he was married... he said he was going to leave her... he said it was a marriage... you know, just on paper... but... he never did. His wife... and him... they bring up my boy... because I... was in a bad place. I was stupid, Tristan, very stupid."

Tristan shook his head. "Little steps... small acorns...you will get there... if you need someone to talk to... I may be <u>old</u>... but I can still listen. Oh... here's your first client. I'll tell her to be gentle with you... don't be alarmed... you will get used to her..."

I waited with trepidation. the door was pushed open and there stood a very tall, immaculately dressed woman with long strawberry blonde hair in tumbling curls.

She pointed at her bag. "Valentino"... I gulped. This was not going to be easy.

"I'm Carina. What you see is what you get. I don't want to see a dimwit who shuffles tarot cards and pretends they know what they are talking about.

Time is money. My business deals are worth millions. I do not mess around. If I like you I'll come back, if I don't... you won't see me again... Where do I sit?"

Carina was a whirlwind of energy. I was terrified, but I had to focus. I could not mess this up. I remembered Almodine was a <u>character</u>, and I was playing her. I tried to be expressionless, not to be intimidated.

"My name is Almodine... is it career or business? I don't use tarot cards, and I am a Psychic, Clairvoyant, Medium..."

Carina took her compact from her handbag and looked at herself in the mirror.

I had to intervene. "Sorry... Carina... I need you to focus so I can maintain a connection with you..."

I closed my eyes... Still Carina was shuffling in her handbag.

"You have been feeling powerless of late... there is a name linked to work... Amanda... there is a significant deal... but there are two clauses you need to watch out for... I am not sure Amanda can be trusted..."

Carina snarled: "No. I am not feeling powerless... I don't know an Amanda... you are not connecting. I'll go..."

I concentrated hard. I needed the money so badly. This was my chance to bring my son back to me. I concentrated with all my strength.

"You had a miscarriage three years ago... Steven... there was a Steven... You fell... there was a stairway... wrought iron balustrade. I see it... you didn't want to tell anyone... but it scarred you... it did... it scarred you..."

Carina's complexion was tinged with grey as she whispered: "How could you know that? I... I... told no one..."

Carina nodded. "You are real. So tell me about Philip in my company."

"Philip is a lying, cheating, snake..."

I stopped. I realised I had overstepped the mark.

Carina smiled broadly. "Hell yeah... you got that right. I need to go... a meeting... but I thank you... you are like me... you say it straight. It's Almodine, isn't it? Good to meet you..."

With a whirlwind she was gone, and I could breathe again.

I could do this. I knew I could.

Chapter Six

It was three cups of tea until my next client. In contrast to Carina, a forlorn looking woman, with cropped red hair and hazel eyes, wore a floral skirt with elasticated waist and frayed hem. Her raincoat had grubby sleeves and her hands looked like they had been itched red raw.

I took the initiative. "Please take a seat... I'm Almodine... Psychic, Medium, Clairvoyant..."

I was interrupted by the woman tapping my arm, "I'm Jeanne... I... just want to know <u>one thing</u> when is he going to leave his wife?

Look at me, soaked through... I walked forty-five minutes to speak to you. My husband doesn't know I'm here..."

I expected to say something but Jeanne kept talking. It was obvious there was no-one else she could trust.

"I met him on a bus... I know you may laugh... not very romantic, is it... all a little bit hopeless I know. He had dropped his wallet somewhere... he had no loose change. I helped him out. I always have change in my purse. You see, I am no-one exciting. I'm just Jeanne, a housewife. Suppose I've let myself go. If I look in the mirror I don't even recognise myself.

It's been twenty years... when his daughter was eighteen he was going to leave, then it was after her wedding day... and he's still with her. I see him every second Saturday. It's not much is it?

Sorry... I've talked too much... they know me here... I never tell my husband I've seen a Psychic. He would say his usual... you'll trip yourself up with all the nonsense in your head, Jeanne."

As Jeanne was talking I knew as sure as sixpence this man would <u>never</u> in a million years leave his wife. How was I going to tell her? As I gazed at Jeanne's pleading eyes... I couldn't do it. I had to go with my gut instinct.

"There is always hope, Jeanne, after all he is making the effort to see you every second Saturday... so... in his heart he... he feels a lot for you... that I know for sure."

Jeanne smiled like a child unwrapping a tinsel bow from underneath a Christmas tree.

"You have made my day, Almodine. You know he loves me?

I nodded. "Yes... he does... he just struggles to show it... He hides behind responsibilities."

I felt I was masking the truth.

Jeanne smiled. "I come here every week. I say I'm topping up the electricity. I suppose I'm not telling a lie... I'm giving myself a battery re-charge.

Do you have time to have a cup of tea, Almodine?"

"Jeanne, this is your reading, don't you have any more questions for me?"

"No love, I just needed to know he still cared... that keeps me going for another week."

I shared a cup of tea with Jeanne. Little did I know she would be one of my most loyal clients.

I didn't want to ever hurt Jeanne, or take her glimmer of hope away. I was no fraud, but I felt truly she had been hurt enough.

My day had gone better than I imagined. The money I had left from Bridget would be used for a bunch of flowers, a jar and a mop and bucket.

It's strange. I hadn't heard from Matty all day, but he had a mysterious kind of existence. I made my way back to the apartment tentatively. I knew what I was facing. It needed more than just a clean; it was really not the kind of place I could take my little boy. It would make them think I was more of an unfit mother than they thought I was.

The stairway to the top floor apartment was dimly lit. I knew I was strong, but I suddenly felt vulnerable. Matty greeted me at the top landing.

"I think I get a sheet of gold stars, your new apartment awaits!"

I think Matty was over exaggerating somewhat. It was still the same downtrodden apartment, but with the addition of a new bed and mattress, a kettle, some plates and a small sofa (that had seen better days).

"I got cleaners in... so it must feel a bit more like home..."

I couldn't be ungrateful... at least it was a new bed, and it did smell clean... really, it was all I could ask for.

This was the start of me changing me. The rope bridge to my son seemed to stretch over mountains, but I had to take each step with courage, even if I was to fall.

Chapter Seven

Matty disappeared as quickly as his words. I lit the solitary candle. The scent of orange peel and cloves filled the room. I could not believe it was only four weeks until Christmas.

There was a tentative knock at the door. I was expecting no visitors... maybe it was a debt collector. I wasn't sure what to do... on the other hand maybe it was Matty.

I opened the door gradually, putting my foot in the door in case I had to slam the door in a hurry to protect myself.

I saw with half my face, a very tall woman holding a large gift bag. Maybe she had come to the wrong door.

"Hi... It's Barb... from next door... I won't hurt you..."

I opened the door, really too tired to make an acquaintance.

"Barb... pleased to meet you... I've made a few sandwiches next door... you know I'm a friend of Matty's... he told me to look after you..."

I forced a smile. Barb had a kind of overpowering energy. I didn't really know what to make of her being so pushy.

"Here's a bag of food love... you know, a few bits and pieces."

I reluctantly followed Barb to the next door apartment. It was like no other apartment I had ever seen. It was gloriously lavish... gilded mirrors that looked Parisian... a beautiful writing bureau that looked as if it was made of walnut with finely polished handles.

"Matty has told me all about you, Jessie... I'm sorry to hear what happened with your little boy. I am sure things will work out... you just need to get yourself on your feet... it takes time."

The room had a scent of opulent incense candles.

"I am a business woman, Jessie. Everything here I have worked for... nothing was given to me on a plate. Some have it that way, but it never helps them. They never succeed. They rarely make anything of themselves as they do not need to try. You see, I understand people."

I could not take my eye off the beautiful paintings that adorned the smooth cream plastered walls.

Barb looked at me intently. "So... how did you meet Matty?"

I suddenly felt violated. I knew nothing about this poised, confident woman but she seemed to know everything about me.

"I met Matty by chance... in a coffee shop... not really much to say, I suppose..."

"One piece of advice.... Matty will promise you the moon and stars... but that's all it is... empty promises."

I didn't want to believe Barb. I felt she had a cold, brittle edge to her, razor sharp in nature.

"Chai tea, dear?"

I politely declined. Barb's intense gaze was almost too much to bear.

"Oh and don't tell Matty about our conversation. What we talk about will go no further, you understand?"

I nodded.

"I understand. Nice to meet you, Barbara."

"Barb, never Barbara. Take care, Jessie, dear."

Chapter Eight

I sat quietly wondering about my little boy. I wondered if he was even remembering my name.

I placed his photograph into a tiny silver frame.

"One day, Noah, I will be able to lift you up and carry you. We can look in all the shop windows, and I will be able to choose a present for you. I will wrap it in bright red and silver paper that will sparkle more than any star in the sky. I think of you when I wake up to the moment I try to sleep at night. We'll be together soon. I know we will."

Just then there was a loud, persistent banging on the door. I hoped it was not Barb with more questions.

"It's me, Matty..."

"How do you fancy a walk to the Ferris Wheel... the fairground is here. Don't ever say I don't spoil you."

I felt tired after the day at Bridget's. "I... I think maybe I should stay in... you know, work tomorrow..."

"What are you, a woman in her eighties? Get your coat on!"

Matty took my hand. "Let's go to the Ferris Wheel, reminds me of being a kid. Candy floss and popcorn and the spinning wheel of lights that ignite you from within. When was the last time you went to the Fair, Jessie."

I smiled. "I took Noah, wrapped up in my arms, just to see the lights... That was just before..."

Matty shook my hand. "Forget all that. It's the here and now that matters."

As we sat on the Ferris Wheel with the wind chilling my nose and ears, I could not help but think if Noah still had his blanket, or if he had any trace of life with his mother at all.

I was not with Matty at all that night, as he shrieked with delight as children laughed. I was crying inside, yet I smile broadly.

"You know, I'll never leave you Jessie, not like Noah's father. It's different, you and me. We understand each other. We don't put pressure on each other. It is what it is..."

I wasn't exactly sure what it was, nor did I care. It was a distraction. I didn't know it then. I thought it was all consuming, but the weight of it's emptiness was like carrying grey granite in my pocket.

The Ferris Wheel turning seemed endless, each time it turned I held my breath. "Take my friendship bracelet Jessie... I knew the first time we met in the coffee shop you were a different type of girl."

"Different?"

"You know, you did not have your claws into me like other girls. You understood me. You did not suffocate me... what's the word I would use..."

I thought for a while... "Empathic."

"Exactly... you are empathic. Actually I was thinking... we could do something different..."

"Different?"

"We could go to a hotel... I have my dad's card... we could get a great room, have some dinner..."

I was astonished. I had not seen this... not seen this at all...

"Matty, this is not a good time for me, you know that...."

Matty paused, and twirled his scarf.

"So... I give you an apartment rent free and you are turning down a night in a hotel... Seriously? I am not talking about a Bed and Breakfast, but a luxury hotel.

Have you looked in the mirror, Jessie? You look exhausted. I feel bad now, for doing you a favour, and I should not feel like that. I should not feel like that at all."

I was the mouse in a game of cat and mouse, where Matty was always going to be the winner.

"Let's do the hotel. It sounds exactly what I need..."

I said the words robotically like I meant them. It was clockwork. I needed that apartment and I needed breathing space.

I got off the Ferris Wheel with legs like jelly. I wish I'd worn a better coat. I had no bag for the hotel stay either.

Matty took control. The doorman seemed to know Matty.

"Hey Matty... you look great... maybe we can meet at the Casino soon..."

I was blatantly ignored by the doorman. I turned my fact away, as I heard laughing.

"How much did she cost you Matty? She's not from the Casino though..."
Matty laughed almost hysterically.

The entrance was garish: lime and raspberry coloured marble pillars, and faded oil paintings that looked glaringly reproduction were nailed to the walls.

Matty seemed to know the brunette girl who handed him the room key, and I stood behind the marble pillar waiting on my fate.

"I ordered dinner for the room... you are not really dressed for the restaurant."

I nodded. I thought the time would go quicker if I said nothing, nothing at all.

"Steak tartare... I love it, a fish stew, and a decent bottle of fizz"

Matty didn't think me worthy enough to look at the menu.

The night was a blur. I thought about Noah, as I tasted the steak tartare and smiled pleasingly. It was vile.

I decided to take control.

"I don't want the fish stew. Let's just go to bed now, that I'll go back to the apartment by myself."

"Jessie... I did not expect that from you..."

"Yes you did. That's why you brought me here..."

Matty's eyes were like a vulture, cold, piercing. He mauled me, but it was quicker because I let him drink the whole bottle by himself. I also was good at closing my eyes so I wasn't really there. I put on my coat, that had a small hole on the left sleeve. I closed the door quietly. The hotel carpet had a smell of shame, more than my hands.

I didn't cry. I clenched by feet in my ill-fitting shoes, and vowed to get out of Matty's apartment.

I was in the gutter but I sure as heck was not going to stay there.

Chapter Nine

Barb was smoking a cigarette outside of her ornate front door.

There was probably mascara running down my face as I clutched Matty's friendship bracelet.

"Cigarette, Jessie?"

"No, but give me a light to burn this bracelet... they are no friend of mine."

"Matty?" I was shocked at Barb's audacity. I could read people I thought, but she had a road map.

"Have you ever been on the Pacific Highway, Jessie?"

I felt uncomfortable. I felt like Barb was acting like a second rate therapist. She constantly talked in riddles that baffled me.

"In California. My good friends bought a farm... more orange trees than the eye can see. Do you know what keeps their heart beating? The Mexican family that pick oranges in the sun that would bore a hole in your soul. My friends do not abuse their heart, their generosity of spirit.

The pickers of fruit give life. They give hope."

"I don't understand what you mean, Barb..."

"Look outwards, Jessie... out of the tiredness that engulfs you... it will be like the orange tree. You will feel the sun again, not today you may think, not tomorrow, yet at the breaking of day the sun still shines bright."

"Matty is just passing through your life, love... don't rely on him. His mother and father know how to turn a coin, but they were born into money. Investments... you know the way. You and I are grafters."

I was intrigued at how Barb seemed to know everything about Matty's life.

"Matty could change... he could grow up. He says he would never leave me like Noah's father. He says one day he would love children... things to be different."

Barb looked solemn. "He's bankrolled on a ticket around the world, a party boy Why would he change for someone like you?"

I had heard enough. "I'm tired. I'm working tomorrow..."

Barb nodded. "The people you read for never want to hear the truth, but they thank you when you do... remember that..."

Chapter Ten

Tristan was waiting for me.

"Today is a busy day for you. News travels fast. You are fully booked."

I was drained, and I really did not want to see Matty. Yet I had to keep quiet. I could tell no-one, though I think Barb knew more than she was letting on.

Tristan looked into my eyes.

"What's happened? You'll get used to being in the new apartment. It all feels new. I'm old, and I find it hard to accept a new china tea cup. I'm just a creature of habit. I still talk to my wife every day, like she is still around me"

"She is still around you, and she says to wear your new glasses, the tortoiseshell ones you don't like. They are in the second drawer of the bureau. Oh, and do you eat scrambled eggs <u>every</u> day?"

Tristan smiled the widest smile.

"How on earth did you know...?"

"She is letting me know you should treat yourself to the painting you saw... the tree house... the golden buttercups... a lovely painting... but over priced she says... you should haggle..."

"Thank you Almodine... I mean Jessie..."

"Anytime I can help, you have been good to me."

"I wondered, Tristan... after work... if you would walk with me to see Noah... in the play ground.... just to see him after school. I just want to see a glimpse of him. I know you probably are too busy, but I could do with... you know... a friendly face..."

Tristan looked surprised. "I will need to look at my extremely busy diary, but I am sure we can find an hour free..."

"Thank you so much... I really appreciate this."

Bridget slammed the door.

"Less socialising you two, there are people waiting. Almodine, brush your hair for goodness sake..."

A smartly dressed gentleman looked tense as I approached.

"Pleased to meet you Almodine. I have heard you are very good. I need clarity. It's been a difficult week."

I tried to slow down my breathing, and take on the calm persona of Almodine, so different from me.. Jessie.

"Your name please?"

"Raymond."

"I want to know if my wife, Narnie, is actually carrying my baby. My gut instinct is telling NO. It doesn't add up... we lived apart for a short while. This is a new start for us, and I do want to be a good father."

I could see Narnie in front of me... petite, large brown eyes, long wavy hair, but anxious. She looked in a mirror, and was talking about Alexander. She had not loved Raymond for a long time, but he was stable. He was reliable. He came home for tea. He was loyal.

Yet Narnie, she wanted more, much more. Raymond made her feel like a loose piece of a jigsaw puzzle. Alexander made her feel younger... However they had been swimming in the sea, it felt all consuming, it felt... true to what she had waited for.

Raymond stared at me, motionless. It was as if he knew. However, what I saw shocked me. Alexander with the most beautiful of eyes... had no money, nothing.

Narnie had to face reality. She did not tell Alexander about the baby to allow him to leave...

I knew that, despite the mundane relationship I could see in front of me, Raymond would be a good father. Narnie would one day learn to love him.

I smiled reassuringly at Raymond. "I see that you should not worry, the baby is yours. Narnie is quiet because she is feeling a little afraid, overwhelmed. All will be well."

Raymond looked shocked. "Are you sure? The baby is mine?"

I nodded.

"Thank you Almodine. I am the luckiest man... I should buy a locket for Narnie... I was holding back... just in case she didn't choose me..."

"Walk with your head held high, Raymond. Narnie loves you..."

I knew I had not done anything wrong. Alexander was only an overhead storm for Narnie. Raymond was the sky. She would realise the day her baby was born, when Raymond was weeping with joy. They would be one."

Raymond turned to look at me before he left. I knew he would be on his way, and he would never need to talk to me again.

I needed a cup of coffee, but that was not to be.

Carina was a woman on a mission.

"I need a Gin and Tonic. Seriously. That useless old man downstairs needs to be in an institution. I mean, really. Forty minutes in that grubby looking waiting room. I could have caught anything! He had the bare faced cheek to offer me a cup of tea <u>without</u> milk as he had just run out of milk. Time is money. This is like a holiday camp for delinquents."

I said nothing. Tristan waved his arms in the background, trying to apologise.

"Please sit down, Carina... you obviously have an <u>urgent</u> question for me. How can I help?"

Carina tapped her hand on my desk.

"<u>You</u> should know, <u>you</u> are the Clairvoyant, right?"

"Carina, I am simply asking so I will have an understanding of the question that may be on your mind."

"Don't play mind games with me, Almodine. We both know why I am here... <u>money</u>. I'm thinking of stringing up a rival for compensation... a snake called Richard. He thinks he has the better of me. What do you see?"

Firstly, I saw that Richard was not a "snake" at all, but exasperated. The fact was Carina was going to go her own way, no matter what I said.

Carina liked the sound of her own voice, and my role as a psychic was simply to agree with her. To give any other opinion would lead to defiance from Carina.

"Let me concentrate, and take a look Carina..."

"I think you are right. Richard is headstrong, competitive, and determined to take the lead in the work place. He is insecure however..."

Carina smiled.

"Excellent. Just as I thought. I had the mark of him... jealous, you know... of my achievements."

"Well, Carina, the message I am getting is... do what you have to do... as you will outsmart him."

Carina nodded in agreement, which I was grateful for.

"What colour of suit jacket should I wear for this meeting? The red or the black? It may sound trivial, but it's important..."

"The red, Carina, definitely the red..."

"That's exactly what I thought... Well I am so exhausted after the waiting room scenario I cannot think what else to say."

I was relieved. I could not help but watch the clock, desperate for a glimpse of Noah.

Bridget wandered through the room without me hearing her feet touch the floor.

"Tristan says he is going to walk with you to see Noah. Don't take offence, my love, but I think you should dress smartly, best step forward.

I want you to buy yourself a new pair of shoes, and new coat. You don't want to look to the outside world like you have given up on yourself. People are cruel. They judge on appearances, always have, always will."

Bridget handed me an envelope.

"Bridget I don't get paid until Friday. I don't want to spend my wage now. I want to be careful... so I can get Noah back. I... I..."

"It's not your wage, but a bonus... for the new clients. They are impressed with you. It's a new beginning for you, love. Grab it with both hands..."

<u>Chapter Eleven</u>

I felt fiercely patronised by Bridget, but I also accepted that I needed her. She and Tristan were the family I had, until I could get Noah back.

Tristan walked through, looking awkward.

"There is a lady desperate for a reading. She has insisted on seeing Almodine..."

"I can't Tristan... we have to walk to Noah's school... I don't want to risk being late..."

Bridget turned to me sharply.

"Send the lady in... Almodine will be happy to do the reading. The sign on the door says open... and that's what we are..."

"But Bridget... I need to walk there... tidy up like you said..."

Bridget glared at me, ashen-faced.

"This is <u>not</u> up for discussion... you will do the reading..."

I slumped at the desk, my heart not in the reading.

A young woman with long perfect blonde hair and checked ice-blue coat walked towards me tentatively.

"I'm not sure why I am even here today... I suppose I am a bit lost. You see, my parents have refused to buy me the car that I wanted after I didn't live life by their rules..."

I could not believe Bridget had made me read for a woman who lived in a gilded cage, and could free herself at any time if she actually wanted to. I took a deep breath.

"Can I get your name please?"

"Natasha... and I am not to be messed with Almodine, or whatever you call yourself. You are nothing but a whore. I am Matty's fiancée... you know that, and you made a play for him."

"Do you like your job Almodine? I hope you value it, because I am going to tear your reputation to shreds... do you understand me? You see, money buys choices. Money buys power. Matty obviously saw you as different in some way... perhaps your psychic super powers, perhaps your audacity to be a fake. Whatever it is... you will not see him again."

I felt my legs underneath the table shake. I needed this job, it was my rope bridge to Noah.

"Matty and I are just friends... no more..."

"The doorman at the hotel told me, because I paid him enough to feed his family for a month. Everyone can be bought Almodine... even you."

Natasha stood up... and looked right through me... like I didn't exist.

I felt a strange sense of calm like she did not matter. Fortunately I had made enough money for the rent of Matty's apartment. If I kept Bridget's new coat money, I could live.

Tristan stood at the door.

"I'm so sorry... are we too late to see Noah..."

My watch had stopped. I had no idea of the time. Tristan shook his head.

"I'm an old man... I suppose I'd be a hindrance to you. I cannot walk fast... you go alone... run... you can still make it..."

It felt too late. It was dark outside. The clock on the wall told me what I already knew. I would be far too late.

"Tristan, it's not your fault... really... another day... Noah doesn't know it yet, but I am fighting... I will not let him go, not ever..."

Tristan put on his camel coloured overcoat that seemed to swamp his tiny frame. His silver hair glistened underneath his trilby hat.

"Do you know what I do when I've had a tough day... I take a short walk to "Fitzpatrick's". It's an old, beat up bar, that has great music... pianists, jazz singers, kids wanting to make it big with their worn out acoustic guitars..."

"I'd love to... I'll get my coat..."

Bridget hollered: "I want to see you early tomorrow... Tristan, be careful on that bad leg of yours..."

Tristan rolled his eyes... and took out a cigar from the inside pocket of his overcoat. "Sssh... She doesn't know I smoke... I told her I'd given up fifteen years ago!"

"Bridget is psychic... she'll know alright... she knows everything..."

Tristan took hold of my arm as we walked down the winding staircase. I could see he was a little unsteady on his feet, but I was not impolite. I did not stare.

"Bridget's trying to look after you, Jessie... She means no harm.. She maybe sees a lot of herself in you."

"I didn't get to see Noah because of her, she blocked my way..."

"She's allowing you to make as much money as you can to have choices Jessie. You cannot see that right now, you are young. You feel like you are being barricaded in... I felt like that..."

"Fitzpatrick's" Bar was a short walk away, and hidden from the street. It was in a basement with a gold, wrought iron spiral staircase.

I could hear the sound of a Saxophonist... and as I walked in with Tristan I felt a million dollars. Everyone seemed to know Tristan, and were nodding, or waving.

The barman knew Tristan and his face lit up.

"Wow... it's been so long... it's great to see you. I must let Narnie know you are here... She is forever asking for you... Is it your usual? What can I get for the lovely lady?"

I had never been called a lovely lady, but the lights were dim in the bar.

"Black coffee, no cream."

The barman shrugged his shoulders, "We don't do coffee... it's against the law... we don't do bad music either..."

Tristan tapped my arm. "They do the best cocktails... or how about a Scotch..."

"Coca-Cola, ice and lemon..."

Tristan laughed: "Bridget's not here you know..."

"We need a table... here for the conversation... you know how it is..."

The barman nodded. "I need a decent conversation myself... round the corner... behind the piano..."

There were old records on the wall, and black and white photographs of singers and musicians I did not recognise.

"I'm thinking of getting someone to bring Noah to me... If I earned enough money I could pay someone to help me, couldn't I..."

"Jessie, you have to get a decent lawyer... it's the only way... there are no shortcuts, and don't even think of running away, because they would bring Noah back, it would make things worse..."

"I'm powerless. I have to sit idle, waiting, while strangers to me make all the decisions for my son.

I cannot be helpless. I cannot sleep at night. I need to get him back... like now."

Tristan listened. I could tell he was thinking.

"My wife and I could not have children, so you might think I cannot advise you but you are on a carousel, and you feel you are spinning but... you need to stay with your feet steady."

I listened. I trusted Tristan, even though I only had known him for several weeks. He was helping me building foundations for my life. He did not seem to judge me.

"Has anyone ever tried to take anything away from you?"

"You are asking a man of my age that question? Of course they have. My wife and I had to live apart... my name is not really "Tristan". I am Jewish. We were forced to un away... but at that time there was bleakness... there seemed nowhere to hide. I saw my mother being taken away.

She was careless. She was seen looking out of a window. It was too claustrophobic for her you see. She did not like being hemmed in, confined spaces. She must have known she would get caught. She... she... opened up the sash window but it was old... heavy big window... so she pushed with all her might... remember, she was like a little bird... we had very little to eat.

It was like a game to me. I was a child. I thought it was kind of like a labyrinth. I thought it was like running from the enemy, and we were invincible. I had a toy car Mama bought me.... the car fell out of my hand when they dragged her to the street, and shot her dead to make an example of her.

They said I was a child who changed. I held on to the toy car, and I would never be parted from it. I still have it, though it smells of blood."

There seemed to be endless silence. The music seemed to stop playing, at least I could not hear it.

I had no idea Tristan had spent his whole life running away from his past like I, with mine.

We sipped our drinks in silence, there was no more to say.

Chapter Twelve

Tristan walked me home to my apartment, and there was a sense of discomfort and awkwardness at me not quite knowing what to say.

The apartment felt intensely cold. I was not sure if it was the apartment, or the fact that I had done so many readings and my energy was drained.

there was knock at the door. I didn't answer. It would be Matty, or Barb, and I was in no mood to see either.

I would have a hot bath, and I would light a candle to regain my energy.

Yet my hands were drawn to Noah's photograph, where I was a proper mother holding Noah, aged two years old, in my arms. I had bought him a nice anorak, and Noah chose the red woollen hat.

It had only been three months without Noah, but he was only five years old. He might forget who I was. It was the uncertainty, the living edge that drove me to find a lawyer that would fight for Noah, and I suppose would fight for me.

I could hear the sound of shouting outside the front door of my apartment. It seemed to intensify. Surely Barb could hear it.

I put on my dressing gown quickly, and tentatively opened my front door. I was shocked to see Barb being held against the wall by two men.

I have no idea why I reacted the way I did, but my gut instinct was to help Barb. I knew she was older than me, but she was also immaculately dressed, perfect. She would never be able to defend herself.

I ran out, mascara running down my cheeks, and shouted: "My husband's on his way... get off her..."

The two stocky looking men in cheap looking suit jackets and smelling of cheap wine and tobacco, glared at me.

"Husband? Who are you kidding? You on the game just like this whore?"

I was stunned. Barb looked terrified, but could not look me in the eye.

"Get your hands off her and I'll give you what you want. I've got money..."

Barb yelled: "Get away from here love, this is not your battle..."

The younger man, with a loose front tooth, smiled at me.

"You're a trollop, but you're young. You'll do..."

The rest was all like a hallucination. I was dragged by my wrists to the apartment while one guy, I think he was older, locked my front door.

Some of it I remember... I was knocked to the ground, and punched so many times my head was like a flurry of how I could make it stop.

My dressing gown was torn off and I remember being spat on. It was their way of exerting their authority. I wanted to vomit, but I had no strength.

I only remember waking up to see barb sponging my face, and looking like a frightened child.

"They raped you, because of me... what the hell am I going to do?"

Barb's crocodile tears were for her business, not for me.

I whispered: "Matty got me an apartment... such a <u>big favour</u> next to a brothel. What did he think of me? He was lining me up for my next big career... a whore extraordinaire. You know what gets to me the most... I cannot tell a soul because I need my son back.

You know what that makes me? It makes me <u>pathetic</u>, that's what it makes me... <u>pathetic.</u>

Chapter Thirteen

I learned something harsh. You can fight other battles, but you have to start with yourself first.

My face was swollen, and bruised. I could not let Bridget see it. I didn't phone in sick, because I was too busy washing the filthy stench out of my apartment.

Barb bought me a hamper, fruit and chocolates from a fancy place. I threw it all in the bin. Barb had lied about her identity. Her designer apartment, her blood diamonds... they were worth nothing to me.

Bridget must have believed something was wrong, and sent one of the other Clairvoyants to my door.

I could not answer. My face told the story.

If I told Bridget the truth she would let me go. I would be seen as too much trouble, a bad lot. I would take as many days as I needed to let the swelling go down.

I had to re-build. As soon as I had bought the new coat I would find a room, anywhere but here. I also needed a new identity. I took a pair of scissors... looked at my ugliness in the small handbag mirror that I owned.

The day I cut my hair was the new beginning!

The day I cut my hair I bought a new coat with the money from Bridget. It was mauve, tweed with a checked design that I chose to make me look more grown up. I saw it in the charity shop window.

An elderly lady with blue tinged hair, said: "A young lady with style. So many people have admired this coat, but I think it must have been meant for you. Oh, and I like your hair... do you cut hair, my dear?"

I felt heartened. Years ago we had a neighbour called Lenara who was a hairdresser and she showed me how to cut a fringe. I suddenly felt like an entrepreneur.

"I like to learn... I hope this coat is lucky for me. Oh, and how much is the little bird brooch... the one on the hat stand over there?"

The lady smiled. "Oh, that brooch is worthless, my dear. It's worth nothing at all. It's yours if you want it."

I fumbled for some money. This was a charity shop after all, and I always paid my way.

As I thanked the elderly lady... I could not help but notice a tattered sign on the door... 'Room available. Light cooking and cleaning duties'.

"Excuse me... the room available. It says apply within... do you know if it is still available?"

"Yes it is my dear, is it for yourself? I am afraid you are only a young girl, there are cleaning duties... and it is an old house... just a little attic room. I miss the company you see..."

I seized the moment. I had to.

"I... I work hard. I am clean and tidy and I don't drink or smoke. I... I... do cook... and I am very good at cleaning..."

The lady looked concerned.

"I have seen that far-off look before... what are you running away from, my dear. It's best you go home... not live with an old dear like me..."

"I... I can't go home, but I am trustworthy. You can give me a trial. A month... if you are not pleased with my cleaning I will go willingly. I am no trouble. I promise you... and I am happy in a small room... <u>really</u> I am..."

"I think everyone deserves a chance, and I think you do have a cheerfulness about you. I'll need references mind, and a month's rent up front, and no visitors."

"Thank you... I am Jessie Lindemann... you won't be disappointed, I promise you."

Chapter Fourteen

It was time to see Matty and hand the keys to the apartment back. I wanted out of there, though the <u>real</u> reason would remain locked inside of me.

I walked to Delaney's with haste. I did not want to be particularly polite to anyone in Delaney's... I did not know who I could trust.

Aoife looked distracted. "I'm waiting on a fruit and veg delivery... and, as usual, it's like a game of Kerplunk. I feel like marbles are falling everywhere."

I did not particularly want to listen to Aoife Delaney talking about marbles, but it would be a waiting game until Matty walked through the door.

I ordered a small coffee, with nothing to eat. I did not need distractions.

Within minutes I could see the silhouette of Matty smoking at the front door. I felt he knew I was here. I could feel it.

Matty pushed the double doors confidently, and his eyes darted around, as if looking for his prey.

"Hey Jessie..."

I did not want to hear the words, "Hey Jessie", or anything from Matty's mouth.

"I am not staying Matty. This is business. I have your rent money, and I have your keys. This is it..."

"Aoife... two coffees... and two bacon and eggs... with toast... and marmalade..."

2Matty, like I say, I am not staying and I don't want breakfast. This is not what you think... me playing hard to get... You <u>lied</u> to me... big time..."

"<u>Lied</u>? Oh, come on Jessie... you've not had enough coffee... you are tired... this is Matty, your <u>good friend</u>, remember? Matty, the guy who rescued you when you were in shark-infested waters?

Did I introduce you to Bridget? Well...? Did I want any praise for that... any recognition? In fact, I asked <u>nothing</u> from you... I gave you a pretty decent apartment which I offered <u>rent free</u>... I mean, what guy would give you all that?"

"Are you serious, Matty? The pretty decent apartment as you call it... is next to a woman who runs a high class Escort Agency, or should I say, in addition... a brothel. You <u>really</u> thought of me, didn't you? The rich kid you are, whose parents have bankrolled countless properties. What do you do...? Give me the bottom of the pile, where the apartment would lie empty anyway.

You lied to me, Matty, but here is your filthy rent money. Give it to your fiancée.

Yes, the fiancée you <u>forgot</u> to mention when you took me to the hotel room to use me as a commodity. You <u>used</u> me when you knew I had lost my son, when I was vulnerable. What does that make you? It makes you lower than the dirt underneath the soles of my feet."

Aoife walked to me, sullenly. "I suggest you leave now, Jessie, before I ask you to leave. Matty has been good to you, buying you coffees and the like... maybe you should remember that..."

I would never walk into Delaney's again. I thought Aoife would have listened to me, but that would never be the case.

I threw the keys and rent money on the table and, like the loser in a small town casino, I left quietly.

I felt surprisingly good walking back to collect my bags from Barb. I felt I had found my voice, even though it was small and faint, it was there just the same.

Barb looked saddened. "Where will you go, love? You know if you need money, I'm here... no questions asked.

I don't want you to take offence, but I noticed your bag. The strap was broken. I have designer handbags... you know, the real deal... I... never use them. I bought them because I could.

I thought this navy handbag was just you... understated but classy... please... take it... I can't take back what happened... I thought we could have been good friends. I am not what I seemed at first. I know I let you down. I should have told you.

If I had told you I had been a prostitute, would you ever have spoken to me? You would have locked the apartment door and never come out to say hello. I wouldn't have expected anything less. Truth is, I am used to it.

I paid off my kids' mortgages, and I have this beautiful villa in Sorrento. I have it all, except you might say, I am still a whore..."

I accepted the handbag. "Barb, this is the most beautiful handbag I have ever seen. I love it, thank you. I mean, I appreciate your kindness. I don't think you do yourself justice, Barb. You are a kind person, and you never asked me any questions on who I was, or where I had come from. You did not judge me. I just... cannot be tied to Matty... I need my independence... I want my son back... every day without him I am failing him..."

"I do not think you will fail at anything you do, Jessie, because you try. You make sure you eat properly now, won't you... and walk with your head held high. It is compulsory. No matter what stones that are thrown at you... keep walking forward."

Barb hugged my like a mother. I had been wrong about Barb. She was just like me. She was just trying to pave her way.

Barb watched me at the top of the stairs while I clutched my new handbag, like it made me much more important than I really was.

I would not realise until later that night that Barb had given me enough money to live on for a year, tucked away inside the bag. There was a tiny note that read:

"Every independent woman needs a chance. Here is yours. Please always see me as your friend. Barb."

This would be my money for the lawyer, not for me. It was the only lifeline I had for Noah, and I was going to grab it.

Chapter Fifteen

It was time to see my second chance: the place I would call home, at least for a little while.

The staircase and steps to the Town House were very grand. The front door was painted the most vivid shade of royal blue. I rang the door bell nervously, no answer. I rang the door bell again... I hoped this was the house... and I had not made a terrible mistake.

I pondered my fate on the doorstep as, sure enough, the lady from the charity shop appeared. She was immaculately dressed with a baby blue cashmere cardigan, floating cornflower blue skirt, and bronze coloured flat pumps. She wore blush coloured rouge, and a dragonfly necklace.

"Lovely to see you, Jessie... please... wipe your shoes on the mat..."

The vestibule was stunning... beautiful Victorian tiles, with not a mark or stain. There was a hat stand, and a picture of a sunset on the wall. It looked like a small oil painting.

"Don't dilly dally, my dear... let me take your coat... I have tea in the drawing room..."

There was a scent of lemon and lavender, and there was a huge staircase with beautiful wooden balustrade. I could not help but stare at the beautiful paintings on the wall. I was in awe.

"Leave your things in the hallway... let's have tea..."

The drawing room was huge, such a stark contrast to the apartment.

"Tea or coffee, Jessie? I bought a little selection of cakes... There is a beautiful French Patisserie down the road... five minutes walk... if you could collect bread and pastries each day I would appreciate it... my legs are not quite as they used to be..."

"Of course... I have the month's rent in advance... in full. I have counted it out three times... cash... in the envelope..."

"I am Golda Schmidt, Jessie... and I take people as I find them. I always have. I appreciate honesty. I don't do lies or cheating. There is enough of that in the world.

Help yourself to a little pastry dear... come on now... we are friends.

You are very young to be out on your own. I imagine things have been a little tricky."

I had to do the unthinkable. I had to tell a bare-faced lie, because I really wanted to stay.

"Oh no... ma'am... quite the contrary. My parents... they are very successful people... they believed I should go out into the world and learn to find my way... you know, earn my own money... do well like them..."

Golda smiled. "I see... so you are travelling... to find yourself..."

At that moment a tiny little photograph of Noah as a baby fell on the floor onto the Persian rug... at my feet. I was quick to put the photograph in my pocket.

Golda reached out her arm... "Aaah... let me see the little one... who is he? Is he a little brother?"

I gulped. I looked up at the ceiling, and unashamedly I told a lie to Golda, who had taken the time to trust me.

"Yes, he is a little brother. I just thought it would be good to carry the picture around... remind me of home..."

Golda nodded. "Always a good idea, to be reminded to home... Now... shall I show you your room?"

I clutched on to Noah's photograph.

"It's three flights of stairs... follow me..."

Golda had laboured breathing as she climbed the stairs. It was like crossing the ocean, it seemed to take a long time.

Finally we arrived at the tiny attic room. The panel door was painted white. There was coombed ceiling and I bent down a little.

It was small, but not too cramped. There were lots of black and white photographs on the wall, and a blue and white painted jug on the window sill filled with fresh lilac.

"I used to use this room as a little store... you know, odds and ends. There is a good view of the garden... so it's not too bad... My mother always loved a view of the garden... I have a little orchard. I love gazing at my lovely apple trees... reminds me of being a little girl. I still feel a little girl inside... even though I have lines on my face. Your spirit... it never changes. It is never destroyed.

I made a list of your cleaning duties. They are not exhaustive. I also expect you to cook, though you will not be required to cook at week-ends. Like I said before, there are no visitors permitted in the house.

You are lucky. The girl that lived in this room had to go home to her family. Her grandmother was very sick. I expect the cleaning to be of a high standard, and fresh vegetables and meat are delivered.

You do have another job I understand, but I expect your priority is to be here.

My son Edward visits now and again. He does have high expectations of people, but he is like his father. I'll never change him. He travels a lot. Business. He does not like noise in the house... very particular.

I'll let you have your own time. Oh... and as you can see, there are valuables around the house... I have an inventory... please do not take offence. We have to be cautious these days."

"Yes, of course, ma'am." I had a feeling Golda was going to be more fierce than I had first imagined.

I would need to have my wits around me for sure. Tomorrow was my first appointment with a Psychologist. I was dreading it. I would need to answer all the questions "perfectly", except I did not know what "perfect" was. I would have to remain calm. Only then would I be able to be "Almodine" again.

I would need to take one step at a time.

The room felt warm, but it felt like I was an intruder. It felt like it belonged to someone else... and I was just passing by.

I could see the garden with the zigzag paving stones, sun dial and rockery. I doubted I would ever have time to sit in the sun. Little did I know, I would have no time at all.

Chapter Sixteen

The day of the Psychologist. The day I would be on the first rung of the ladder to get Noah back - or not.

I was up at five a.m. I could not sleep in the attic room. The wind rattled in the embers, like a snake in the undergrowth. I felt there was someone at the window watching me. I felt an eerie presence. I blanked it out however, staring at the ceiling until it was time to get up and make breakfast.

I washed quietly, and tiptoed down the stairs to make breakfast for seven a.m. as requested. I would clean the kitchen first, as Golda's instructions stated. I was not expecting Golda to be already sitting at the oversized dining room table waiting for me.

"Excuse me, Jessie... can I see your hands first before you prepare my food?"

I was horrified, and felt my hands shaking. I felt my every movement would be scrutinised.

"Scrub your nails... not acceptable..."

I wandered to the kitchen feeling confused on why I had trusted an elderly woman I had only just met. My gut instinct was obviously wavering.

"The fruit must be sliced, Jessie... and my yogurt in a separate bowl. Can you bring my Earl Grey tea immediately, please... and go and see if my newspaper has been delivered.

I hastily ran to the front door... there was no newspaper.

There is no newspaper yet..." I hollered.

I quickly scrubbed my nails as commanded... and started to cut the fruit, but with my hands shaking the fruit became pulp and not as I would have liked for the presentation.

I knew I had to hurry as I had to walk to the Psychologist office and be on time. I could not look unreliable or reckless. I would then have to see Bridget, and explaining myself was not going to be easy. Bridget may ask me to leave without explanation. I could not think that way. I had to think one step at a time today.

I trembled as I took the breakfast on a silver tray.

Golda looked solemn, ashen faced. In fact, she looked completely different to the woman I had first met.

Golda picked up the silver spoon from the tray and threw it at my feet.

"The spoon is not clean", she screamed. "Open up the drinks cupboard, and bring me the bottle of red wine that is sitting at the front, with a glass... now..."

"But, ma'am... it's the morning..."

Golda stood up, almost spitting at me.

"I pay you a wage to do as I say. Your opinion is not required. Do as I say."

I ran to the cupboard and brought the wine bottle and glass, feeling I was part of a nightmare. I wanted to run, but I had nowhere to go.

"I like the fine things in life, and I am entitled to do so. You will probably never be able to dream of buying a bottle of wine of this vintage, and I suppose you would not want to..."

I kept quiet. I knew better than to try to answer. I looked at the clock on the wall.

"I have an appointment. I shall clean the kitchen... and I shall be back this afternoon..."

Golda stared ahead as she drank her first glass of wine, seemingly oblivious to what I was saying.

Unbelievably I was late as I ran to the Psychologist's office. I weaved my way in between crowds of people, hoping I could not be seen as completely erratic.

My palms were sweaty as I eventually discovered number twelve, with the black glossy door. There was a security door.

"Jessie Lindemann... apologies, I'm late..."

The door opened and an elderly receptionist with blue tinged hair and no smile barely looked up from a stack of uneven papers on her desk.

"Name?"

"Jessie Lindemann"

"You are late. Take a seat. You will be seen."

I sensed a conversation about the weather was not going to happen.

There were old magazines on a glass coffee table, magazines about the countryside, fishing and bird watching. The magazines were at least a year out of date. This did not bode well.

I tried not to look at the clock... but my eyes were constantly fixed on the wall, and the tired looking yucca plant that had seen better days.

At last... forty five minutes later... a poker-faced silver haired gentleman walked through to the reception area. His suit jacket looked two sizes too big, and his spectacles were on blue elastic around his neck.

"Miss Jessie Lindemann please..."

The gentleman did not speak. There was quiet, uneasy quiet as we walked through to his office.

I felt sick, very sick. There were metal bars on his window, and his rectangular desk was untidy with a strange plastic pyramid ornament, and an old fashioned black telephone. It felt bleak.

The gentleman read through what looked like notes... lots of notes...

"So... Jessie Lindemann... I am here simply to ask you a few questions. This is not a test. It should not take too long..."

"Will I be able to see Noah soon, you know, properly, just me and Noah?"

I got no reply. None at all.

"So how are you today, Jessie? How has your morning been?"

I paused... what should I say? I could not tell a Psychologist I had met an old woman, found an attic room and it was disastrous, nor could I say I worked as a Psychic or he would ask me to look for "rainbows" and I would never see Noah again. I decided to say as little as possible.

"Good. I am good, thank you."

"I am Mr Wright. Your name, Lindemann... is that your marital name?"

"I have never been married..."

There was a pause. "You were unmarried when you gave birth to Noah... I see."

I did not like this line of questioning at all. I felt I was going to be backed into a corner like a circus animal.

I felt this man had made up his mind. This was the beginning of Noah being taken off me for good. I felt it. I sensed it. I could not get angry. I had to remain calm. I had to. Otherwise, like a pack of cards falling down, the game would be over.

"Noah's father... Who is he?"

I gulped. My legs were shaking. I would never reveal the identity of Noah's father.

"Eh... I don't know..."

"Interesting... you don't know. Any reason why?"

"I can't remember... I was young... one night... that is all..."

"I see... There is no father's name on his birth certificate?"

"No."

"Your parents, were they happy at your pregnancy?"

"No."

"They were <u>not happy</u>?"

"No".

"They voiced their disapproval?"

"Yes."

"How did they voice their disapproval?"

"They threw me out when I was pregnant..."

"threw you out... that seems very drastic... Was there any other reason they threw you out of their home?"

"No."

Notes were being scribbled on every word I spoke. I tried to keep focused. I was in a labyrinth, in the maze of works and thoughts and actions, but unable to move.

"So... going back to when you were pregnant, Jessie... how did you feel about being pregnant?"

"Eh... I felt... happy."

"Let me get this right... At sixteen years old... at school... you felt happy?"

"Yes... I mean no... not exactly like that..."

"Is the answer yes or no?"

"I... I... I suppose, yes..."

"You <u>suppose</u>?"

I... I... mean <u>definitely</u> yes..."

"So, at sixteen years old, in the middle of your exams, you felt happy... to be having a baby... when you don't know who the father is... you feel happy?"

"Yes."

"There was <u>no</u> contact at this time with your baby's father?"

"No."

"Let me get this right. During your pregnancy there was <u>no</u> contact with your baby's father? None?"

The words were jumbling around inside of me. I felt wobbly. I felt scared, unsure and trapped. It was then that I lost my composure.

"You are <u>twisting</u> it."

"I'm sorry?"

"You are a cold and calculating, heartless, know-it-all and you are twisting it like a knife... you are trying to blame me..."

"Blame you... why would I be doing that? I am a professional, Jessie. I am only here to assist you..."

"No you are not. You are here to assist Social Services to take my son away from me. My son, that I love more than anything in the world. I have done nothing wrong. I have never harmed Noah. I ran out of electricity. I asked for help. I needed somewhere better to stay. I asked for help... and it comes to this... it spiralled out of control to this..."

"What do you mean, spiralled out of control... in what way exactly?"

"All this... Noah with strangers... this... "

"Do you feel Noah should not be with a foster family?"

"No."

"Why not?"

"Noah deserves better..."

"Could you always heat your flat when Noah lived with you, Jessie?"

"Yes... I could..."

"You said earlier you ran out of electricity... Do you think Noah would be afraid of the cold and darkness?"

"No, he was with me..."

"You think Noah would be <u>happy</u> in the cold and dark?"

"I... I... don't know. I love Noah... I... I... don't know..."

"I am here to talk about <u>you</u> and <u>Noah</u>. That is all."

"You are trying to catch me out..."

"Catch me out implies you have something to hide..."

"That is <u>ridiculous</u>. I have nothing to hide, nothing..."

"On a scale of 0 - 10, how honest would you rate yourself on that scale?"

"Ten, very honest..."

"Ten."

"Yes."

"I don't think I would rate myself as a ten... that would mean <u>perfect</u>. No one is really that honest, all of the time, are they Jessie?"

"I am..."

"Are you...?"

"Yes, I am... <u>always</u>."

"Thank you, Miss Lindemann. That will be all today."

"I don't understand. What happens now?"

"I will be seeing you for another few sessions..."

"What does that mean exactly? Can you tell me when I will get Noah back? Do you know?"

"I have no power in that decision..."

"Yes you do... your words mean everything... I know that."

"What are you most afraid of, Jessie?"

"Everything... I am afraid of <u>everything</u>."

Chapter Seventeen

I had no time or inclination to worry about a Psychologist.

I could worry about that tomorrow. Today I wanted to see Noah, just from a distance. I just wanted to see him run, jump in the school playground. I wanted to see him safe, even for a few minutes.

I walked hurriedly, pushing my hat over my ears so Noah would not recognise me.

First I visited the small artisan bakery where I would take Noah for a biscuit, and he would proudly carry it in his hand in a small paper bag. It looked enormous in his tiny hands.

The lady in the bakery recognised me instantly.

"Oh, just on your own today. Where is the little one?"

I fumbled in my purse for loose change.

"He's on holiday..."

The lady smiled.

"Oh, where?"

"I... I... just by the sea... for a few days..."

I paid for the gingerbread biscuit and left quietly.

Lying seemed to be my middle name these days.

For once I was early. I could see Noah... from a distance... but he was dressed differently. It was a different coat... different shoes... and what looked like a different school bag.

I felt confused. I thought everything would be exactly the same. I was shocked. I should have been excited, but I felt cold.

I was so busy looking at Noah running in all directions in the playground, that I was oblivious to some of the other mothers that had swarmed like ants, nearly blocking my view.

"Look at her... Jessie Lindemann... what a bare-faced cheek... dumps her son... and has the nerve to stand near the school gates..."

"I heard she had a nervous breakdown... She tried to cut herself... and the boy was not even fed properly. She moved that boy around like a gypsy, and he never had a bit of stability. She only cares about herself that one..."

"She is all over the place I heard... was crying in a supermarket... Shame for the boy..."

My instinct told me not to approach Noah. Instead, I tapped one of the other mothers on the shoulder,

"Excuse me... would you give this to Noah please?"

The woman smiled meekly, "Of course."

She didn't ask me how I was, even though we had seen each other at the school gate many times. I knew I didn't belong, but I had seen Noah. How could his appearance have changed in such a small time? I didn't understand. It was like they were all trying to erase my part in Noah's life.

It was like I was not considered as being a mother anymore. I was lost. It seemed more lost than before.

I walked away, and I felt out of balance. My legs hurt. My arms hurt. I <u>had</u> to be strong. I had to. No one else was going to lift me up but me.

It is just as well I left so I did not overhear the words.

"I would bin that paper bag. You never know where it's been."

Little did I know from the moment the Social Worker took Noah away, he would receive not a card or gift from me.

Sometimes I think that is why I liked the darkness. I only cut myself once. I felt elated when the blade was dragged along my arm. It felt like I was being heard. I was in control, not other people. When it bleeds, you stop crying.

Cutting once means that they think you will cut a million times. It's how they think. Psychologists work on patterns, likelihood, what you have done or might do. It's how they think.

The only place where I felt I could not be judged right now was with the woman I had initially mistrusted: Barb.

It was also good for me to revisit the apartment. I could not really remember the attack. It was a mirage. A still, black and white picture that happens to someone else.

Walking up the apartment stairs I could smell the pungent cologne.

Barb looked shocked to see me standing at the door.

"Jessie, oh my goodness... I never thought I'd ever see you again... let's get a cup of tea..."

I felt I could breath again.

"Noah looks different... they are changing him... I think they are going to take him away from me permanently. I feel it."

"Come on now love... you are his mother. They cannot do that... you are getting yourself on your feet... look at you... I mean you have a room in a large Victorian mansion... lah-di-dah... what more do they want?"

"It's just a pity the woman in the Victorian mansion wants a dogsbody and a punch bag... that's what she wants."

"I didn't want to put you off, Jessie... but these wealthy, well to do lot... they pay a pittance and expect everything in return... Been there, love.. it's how the world works."

"It's so unfair, Barb... She criticises everything."

"You need to learn to <u>ignore</u>. Think of the sun, the moon, anything, but don't let her empty words sink in... She has no hold on you and she never will have. You know this.

You, Jessie Lindemann, are not a pure diamond... you are a <u>blood diamond</u>... Unusual, sought after, strong... and a blessing.

Blood diamonds shine in mud. They shine through it all. Remember that."

Barb sat slumped, staring above my gaze.

"The first time I was with a man for money, I made a mistake. I was still me... I thought I should try to love the man. I was young and I was stupid. The minute he gave me the money was a business transaction. It was like a trigger... you take money... you switch off.

As I got confident, and was well-known, the money got bigger. I loved the scent of the money, feeling it in my fingers. I used to lie down and think of the places I would go, and the properties I would buy. You see... I needed more houses to feel safe. This was my way out of the gutter and I had to embrace it."

"Were you scared, Barb?"

"Yes... sometimes I was... but I never showed it in my eyes. You never let them in... you have to do exactly the same. Build a wall around yourself so nobody can hurt you... ever. You build the foundations and the walls and each day the cement... it hardens. You may harden your heart, and that is the price... but who else is going to help us but our independent selves?

Women have a right to be independent. If they choose not to be, they let down themselves... no one else... themselves..."

Chapter Eighteen

Barb was right. Barb was always right, though it pained me to admit it. I had to stay focused and close my eyes shut if it all got too much.

It was time for me to face Bridget. What on earth was I going to say to a woman who could read minds? What was she going to say? More importantly, what was I going to say?

I didn't really have time to think about Golda's demands. Bridget was giving me my chance to break free, and I had abused her kindness.

I adjusted my hair nervously, took a deep breath and leapt up the steps to see Bridget, two at a time before I would change my mind.

Tristan greeted me at the door, but he looked different... tired... strained. I knew he was an elderly man, but his face captured youth. His eyes were young, thoughtful and sparkling, but not today. I felt Tristan sensed my apprehension. He didn't even stand to greet me. Only a wall of silence.

I tried to maintain his eye contact. "Tristan... I am sorry..."

"Sorry... what are you sorry for... I take you to a Jazz club... I try to let you see another side of life... and, hey presto... nothing. You don't go missing for hours or days, but weeks... what was I to say to myself... huh?

Has Jessie got caught up in a brawl. Has she been hurt? I walked to all of the hospitals on foot... to be there for you... so you would not be without family, except you were not in <u>any</u> hospital, nor anywhere to be found.

You can <u>hate yourself</u> if you want, but do not ever hate me. I am an innocent here. I thought we were going to look out for each other..."

I stared at the wall, turning my back on Tristan. "I am here now... I am fine..."

"I... I... I... Jessie... what about us that gave you the lifeline you needed? Bridget didn't say much at all, but then she connects with you without words or pictures. I will let Bridget know you are here."

"I... I... cannot see Bridget now... I can another time... but."

Tristan stood up, even though his legs were visibly shaking.

"No. You will see Bridget now, and you will have the courtesy and old-fashioned manners to do so."

I knew Tristan was right, but I had not envisaged his coldness. I had no idea how my disappearance had caused such chaos.

There was a pause, a stillness. I sat slumped on the burgundy velour high backed chair, usually reserved for waiting clients.

I could hear every heartbeat of the ticking clock. It must have been twenty minutes or so... and Bridget stood at the top of the stairs, her face sullen and expressionless. I could not read her.

"It better be good. My office... now..."

It felt like school on a bad day, not that I actually knew school very well.
We moved around a lot.

Bridget pulled her desk slightly closer to her, to create a barrier. No-one
spoke. It was a bubble of emptiness.

"You blew your chance with me, and I don't do chances. I took you on
face value, even though you had nothing to offer but your intuition, and
you tore up my gratitude, into tiny pieces, into shreds.

You are lucky, Almodine. I could never read nor write. We were never
encouraged. We were raised to clean the house, be as beautiful as you
can to catch the carp... a husband. If you were not married by twenty-one
then you were no good to man nor beast. You were on the scrap heap.

We were raised to clean until your fingernails bled. Good little traveller
girl I was. I met him when I was fifteen, he beat me till my kidneys were
pulp but he kept my face clear so no-one would see.

He used to put a handful of nails beneath my feet and ask me to stamp on
them. I married him in the church, and my gown was the most exquisite
dress you would ever imagine. My daddy worked for years with his bare
hands to pay for that dress in cash.

I could take the beatings. I just imagined I was somewhere far off... a
distant city where I could hide... where no-one would know me.

Ten years I was married, and the money I made sewing curtains and altering coats paid for his drink. I handed over every penny to him, and someone helped me. Someone I could not see.

You see, my husband got too clever. He hit my head against a wall and I was so numb that I slid down and was found by strangers. He must have run away when he saw me out cold. He didn't want the blame on his doorstep. He didn't want his precious family name ruined.

That was the start of my new life. I am not Bridget by birth name, but it is who I am now that matters. Nobody has the right to take that away from me.

This business is not just about the money, to turn a coin. It's who I am. It's my family. Tristan has seen it all. When I started here I could hardly pay the business rent. We only put the heat on for some clients.

I thought you understood us. I thought wrong."

My hands felt drenched in sweat. My jaw was clenched.

"I take it you need money, Almodine. How much do you need... and then you can be on your way."

"I didn't come in for money, Bridget. I hoped I could get my old job back... I had things to deal with."

"Things? How do I know when other things happen you won't disappear again... I cannot, or will not, take another chance..."

"Bridget, I had to see a psychologist about Noah... I had to get a new place... I am going to get assessed constantly... my own <u>son</u>. I think they are building a case that I am not good enough..."

Bridget looked at me squarely. "You are <u>not</u> good enough, you hear me? You need a damn good wage each week to prove you deserve your boy back... until then... you are a drifter... your life is questionable. Only <u>you</u> have the answer, Almodine."

"Please, Bridget... I need another chance".

I got down on my knees as if I was in church. I was desperate. My pride was hurled out the window.

"Get up, Jessie... you have been watching too many Vaudeville shows... get up... and save the meagre excuses. You start Monday, nine a.m. <u>on</u> <u>time</u>. You understand? This is not because I am a soft touch, it's because Tristan persuaded me, so thank him, not me. Get out of my sight."
I turned to thank Bridget as I was leaving. "Thank you Bridget... thank you."

Tristan said nothing as I quietly walked to the vestibule. He was fixing a small pocket watch and didn't lift his head as I left.

Chapter Nineteen

Bridget was proud. I could see that, maybe she saw a younger version of herself in me, even though I was yet to prove my worth.

I walked slowly to the place that I was supposed to call home. I wondered where Noah was sitting, or looking out the window, or drawing the pictures with even the broken crayons.

I wanted to buy Noah some new crayons and, without thought, I did.

The tiny toy shop was filled with treasures, and I imagined Noah holding my hand tightly and pointing to the big red car in the window. I tried to imagine Noah with me... I really tried... but try as I might, I could not see him. I wondered if this was a sign that Noah was forgetting about me.

The lady smiled and took the crayons and the drawing book.

"How much is the red car in the window?"

The lady whispered, "It's probably a little more than you would care to pay... but there is a good little shop down the road, on the corner... lots of second hand cars."

I felt deflated. I didn't want a second hand car for Noah. I wanted a brand new shiny car in a big, big cardboard box, taller than he was. I wanted the best that money could buy, but I looked wrong. I _felt_ wrong.

I wanted to buy the pair of scissors next to the crayons and cut myself until my arms felt raw. I wanted to cut myself now.

"Are you alright dear Do you want a little paper bag for the crayons?"

"I will leave the crayons today, thank you... I shall try the second-hand shop down the road... thank you."

The chime signalled at the door. I would take my business elsewhere. Besides, Golda would surely have her list of demands.

I loved the walk to Golda's house. The tree lined avenue with the beautifully kept town houses with wrought iron balustrades, and fancy painted doors with polished brass name plaques. A place I could really only dream of.

I imagined that one day I would have enough money to take Noah's hand, and show him where we would both live, with the biggest, fanciest garden, with a maze, and roses, rhododendrons, and birds that would not be afraid to fly.

I did not imagine I would bring Noah into the world in hiding. I didn't think... I imagined that I could shape the future into something different.

I remembered the words: "Jessie... you know I don't love you... it was a mistake. I am not hurting you. I am being truthful with you, and if nothing else, you should thank me for that."

That was the day I was supposed to tell him I was pregnant. To this day I haven't told him. I decided to be a <u>mother</u>. I decided it was my destiny. It was who I was supposed to be.

The steps to Golda's front door seemed winding, tougher to climb.

I tiptoed across the pristine mosaic tiles... I peered into the drawing room... and Golda was sound asleep in her plush armchair of mauve brocade.

It was time to cook to earn my keep. It would be the moments of calm I would treasure...

Chapter Twenty

I poached my fish, and peeled my artichokes for decoration like I was cooking for a Persian queen.

Golda was strangely quiet as I served the fish with no idea what reaction I would receive.

"Sit with me awhile, child."

I was not a child, but I dared not correct Golda.

"My husband used to love poached fish and rice with turmeric. He travelled to India you know. A learned, intelligent man... he would have treasure troves of teas and spices shipped here. Delicate to the eye."

I smiled politely and cast my eye along the white table cloth to ensure everything was just so.

"Have you travelled to India, Jessie? They say that if you have not walked barefoot in India, then you have not lived at all."

I had barely travelled even to the waterside, but I eagerly anticipated that I perhaps would one day... so I used my imagination. I felt Golda would appreciate a good story.

"Oh yes... though I do find travelling quite exhausting. My parents believed that watching the sun rise in the far-off lands changes you."

"Indeed... So where have you travelled?"

"Mmm... Milan... Salzburg... restaurants in the South of France... oh and Singapore... Dubai, perhaps in June..."

"You travel light for one so well travelled..."

I crossed my fingers underneath the table. Singapore was a step too far... I could not risk being caught out.

"I do hope your fish is delicious, just some lemon... and some capers..."

"The fish is very nicely cooked... travel can be over-rated I find, do you agree?"

"Yes... I mean, No... I mean, I agree with you..."

Golda sat up in her chair. "Your parents do know where you are, Jessie? You have not run away?"

I laughed heartily. "My parents, they speak to me every day. This is just a vacation. We all need vacations..."

I did not look Golda in the eye, which surely meant I was not lying.

"I have son called Edward. He has done very well you know... internationally renowned lawyer, accomplished pianist, loves art galleries... I am sure you will meet him... though he has very <u>exacting</u>

standards. He is engaged to a lovely girl called Fleur. She works in her father's law firm."

"Oh, when do they get married? You must be so proud..."

Golda looked awkward. "Fleur says she does not want to get married in this country. She thinks it is too common place. She wants an intimate ceremony by the sea... but exclusive... a tiny island... her father owns property."

Golda looked desperately sad.

"I have rice pudding... and home-made strawberry jam."

"I am not fit for the wedding dear... and old woman like me...

Without thinking, I reached over and took her hand.

"I would go with you... if you needed me... it is your son. I can only imagine how you feel..."

Golda looked at me sternly.

"Are you going to get the rice pudding before it is inedible... you talk too much child..."

Golda would throw me out of the house if she knew I had a son and nothing to show for being a mother. I would have to talk less.

Golda did not want to talk anymore that evening. Instead her rice pudding remained untouched.

"Best for you to retire early to your room as you have an early start..."

My room did not feel my own. It had an air of sadness... a stillness... the rows of framed black and white photographs so perfectly placed. They were strangers that I did not know, and they did not know me.

I wondered what they would think of me staying there... fractured pieces of belongings. Maybe nobody would know I existed.

Golda was a mysterious woman who was so whimsical yet austere. She was every contradiction you could imagine. Every day that I would stay with her, I would know her less and less.

As I tried to go to sleep... I could hear the sound of a doorbell repeatedly ringing... whoever was at the door was persistent... as they kept ringing... Golda had obviously no intention of answering the door.

I thought it would not be advisable to turn up at the door of a virtual stranger's house with my dressing gown. So I quickly grabbed my vintage lemon tea dress that I wore to work and quickly tied my hair up, to look vaguely presentable.

I ran down the stairs... and quickly answered the door, and was greeted by a very tall, dark haired gentleman with a trilby hat and very smart pin-stripe suit, carrying a suitcase and several bags. He looked at me up and down: "Who the hell are you?"

I tried to pull my stomach in and stand taller. "I am Jessie Lindemann. I live here..."

"My name is Edward and no, you <u>do not</u> live here... I do... get out of my way..."

"Can I take your bags, Edward? Have you been on a long journey?"

Edward looked at me in horror.

"Get out of my way... where is my mother... where is she?"

Edward pushed past me in a rage, and his strained footsteps echoed on the old Victorian tiles in the vestibule.

Golda was slumped in an armchair with a glass of brandy, and her reading glasses perched on her nose. Her paperback book lay on the floor with ripped out pages strewn all over the floor.

"I <u>used</u> to like this book Edward... now I <u>hate</u> the damn book."

"Have you been drinking, mother?" Where did you get the drinks cabinet key...?"

I knew I was watching an awkward conversation but I had to fight for my right to stay. I had to work, and I had to have a roof over my head for me... then for Noah. Golda had not been drinking when I had left her.

"Can I get anyone a cup of tea or coffee... or maybe some sandwiches?"

Edward turned on me.

"Are you a thief, or are you plan stupid... did you find the drinks cabinet key?"

Golda stuttered...

"Leave the girl alone, Edward... you cannot come in here throwing your weight around... I have not seen you in months... so I had every right to change the locks if I want to..."

Edward looked at me menacingly: "Pack your bags and get out. I have seen your type before... an opportunist... preying on an old lady who is vulnerable..."

Golda stood up and threw her brandy glass against the fireplace, shattering the glass into tiny pieces.

I leapt forward: "Be careful... you could cut yourself ma'am. I will clean everything up for you..."

Edward watched me motionless as I cleaned up the pieces of glass and wrapped them in a napkin.

"Bring a pot of coffee, Jessie. Edward, this is Jessie my cleaner, cook and companion."

Edward shook his head. "I do not need meaningless introductions. None of your other staff have lasted five minutes, this one won't either..."

I quietly carried the broken glass, and realised Edward's sudden unannounced arrival did not spell stability for me. I was on a capsized boat, and the water was seeping in... from everywhere.

As I walked to the kitchen the pieces of broken glass suddenly felt good in my hand. I felt safe, like I could cut myself all over and no-one would notice. I was so tempted. I threw the glass in the bin, and washed myself again and again and again, repeatedly drying myself.

I carefully carried through a pot of coffee and some biscuits while Edward watched my every move.

"I want to see papers... your I.D... where you came from... references... can I see those now?"

"It's late at night Edward.. I have seen all the references and, in case you haven't noticed, this is my house not yours. Go to your room, Jessie, thank you. Breakfast as usual... and go upstairs... we are all good..."

I closed the drawing room door, but waited to hear if I would be leaving tonight.

"I want to see those references mother. She looks like a gypsy that sort. I mean, can she even read or write? What is she exactly? How did you meet her?"

"Edward... you need to stop being to judgemental. The girl needs this job and she works hard. I have no interest in anything else. Give her a chance. Besides, why are you here Edward? More money from your father's estate? You did not come to visit me, so why are you here?"

"Fleur said I should visit you more... and so I thought I would surprise you..."

"Edward, you are <u>my son</u>, you don't do surprises. You mean Fleur and you had another row... so you find some refuge with your old mother. Am I right?"

I could hear footsteps, so I ran to my room, but kept the light on all night. The uneasiness I felt in my room, and after making breakfast I had to face Bridget.

Chapter Twenty-One

I didn't sleep that night, worried that Edward may ask me to leave during the night against his mother's wishes. It was obvious to me Edward had his own agenda.

I prepared Golda's breakfast carefully and diligently. I did not expect to see Edward, immaculately dressed in his suit, drumming his fingers on the table.

"Do you have any kippers for breakfast? I feel like kippers... and <u>decent</u> coffee. I do not do cheap coffee, and it must be freshly ground..."

I kept a sense of calm. "I have smoked salmon, eggs, porridge, muesli... and, of course, fresh coffee..."

"No... I feel like kippers. If I ask for it, I expect it. You <u>work</u> here, so get some kippers and cook them... simple."

Fortunately for me Golda intervened. "Enough of the petulance Edward. You can have smoked salmon..." Jessie, you can leave now."

Edward sighed and as I left quickly to be early for Bridget, Edward followed me.

"I see you have your feet under the table here with my mother... but not with me. I will <u>tolerate</u> you for my mother's sake, but we all know she is losing it. She has never had any common sense since my father passed...

you <u>see</u> that of course. You are a smart girl obviously... streetwise. You tell people what they want to hear but you obviously are desperate if you chose to live here with a narcissistic drunk.

"I don't think you should disrespect your mother like that. She does not deserve it..."

"I don't believe your name is Jessie. I don't believe your fairy tales like my mother. You are seeing what you can get out of it, and perhaps I cannot blame you. It's all free will after all. I will give you a piece of advice, you will never change my mother, so don't even try. She will drive you away, just like she did me."

I had no time to spend listening to Edward's venomous words, so dropped my head and pretended to be compliant. It was easier. Besides, Bridget would not allow me to break her trust again, that I knew for sure.

Chapter Twenty-Two

I did not think of Edward's untimely arrival, nor did I think of the fact that Golda could be persuaded to ask me to leave. I thought of only one thing: Noah. I was an empath, so I knew he was secure. Did I think of his happiness? I did... but not too much... for if I did... I would surely haunt myself.

Before I would face Bridget, and the pain I had caused Tristan, I saw the beautiful old church that sat majestically at the top of a winding labyrinth of steps. It seemed fitting that I light a candle for Noah, and one for my strength. Resilience and strength are different, but resilience seemed the easiest to contemplate. Strength seemed harder.

Walking up the uneven, worn steps... I wondered who had walked the same steps before me, and what was their journey.

The dark brown, heavy door to the church looked firmly closed, but I gently pushed... and it revealed just as I imagined... the most exquisite tiles that were like hushed whispers of hope.

I was alone in the church, though that felt right. It was dim in the sense of no lights, but the beautiful purple, scarlet and gold stained glass windows lit my path to light a candle.

As I walked slowly and reverently I suddenly felt I was a failure. The realisation that I had pushed to the back of my mind was right in front of me. My hands trembled as I lit the candle. It flickered, but did not go out.

It seemed right to talk out loud, and I did not feel afraid to be myself.

"Noah, wherever you are, I did not leave you. I will get things sorted out. One day we are going to have a big house... and we can play in the garden. I will buy you the biggest climbing frame, or maybe a tree-house, and we can laugh and sing. It <u>will</u> be different. I <u>promise</u> it will. I just need some more time..."

I could hear footsteps though when I turned around, there was no-one to be seen. It seemed right that I go to Bridget's early, and be prepared. What I was not prepared for was the visitor that would greet me, as I ran to Tristan.

"Jessie Lindemann, we have been trying to contact you for several days... Noah has asked repeatedly to see you... and we and the foster parents believe that it is in Noah's best interests for you now to have some quality time together... and perhaps make him feel a little bit secure... your residential address details do not seem up to date. I think this weekend... Saturday or Sunday, Jessie? Noah has been becoming unsettled as he has had no idea of your whereabouts, and it seems you have been off the radar."

Bridget walked to her desk briskly, and it seemed deliberately interrupting.

"Jessie has been an exemplary employee, working here on a full time basis. I am happy to complete any necessary paperwork. I understand for people such as <u>yourself</u> it's all about the paperwork, isn't it? Oh, and Jessie resides with me... the Orange Tree development... Yes, my property was designed by Lucas Peterson, the Architect. Beautiful. You love it, don't you Jessie... very tranquil... wonderful place for Noah to visit at the weekend."

The Social Worker looked deflated, while Bridget smiled broadly.

"People call it Millionaire's Row... but that is just shameful, isn't it. Some people think that money can buy power or status... and I suppose it's just like those that look down on young Jessie there..."

The Social Worker coughed uncontrollably.

Bridget leaned over her: "Glass of water dear... I don't judge anyone, love, but I suggest you take your clipboard and your checklists... as you will need them for Court. Jessie is a fine mother. Now, off to your work Jessie... We don't do shenanigans around here Tristan, do we?"

Tristan shook his head, trying to keep composed.

"No, we do not. Some people would see Social Workers as prepped up administrators but not us, Bridget... not at all..."

The Social Worker stood up: "I had no idea that Jessie was residing at Orange Tree development... no idea at all..."

Tristan walked slowly to the door: "Let me see you out, Madam... and may I with you a good day..."

The Social worker looked stunned. "This is very unorthodox... Jessie gave us a totally different address..."

Tristan shrugged his shoulders. "Perhaps... your administrative error...?"

I peered around the corner: "Has she left yet, Tristan?"

"The coast is clear... the tyrant has left the building, and I am not sure she will be as sure of herself as when she walked in for sure..."

I ran to Tristan and gave him the small prayer card I had collected in the church. "Thank you... for believing in me... and for the second chance."

"You know, Jessie, I wasn't always this pathetic old man, hobbling along with my bad hip and pains in the leg. When I was your age I was a gambler. I used to play Baccarat... I was an observer at first... but then I watched the rollers... how they held themselves... and do you know what I learned, Jessie?"

I was stunned. I did not see Tristan as a gambler. I saw him as careful, considered, learned... everything a gambler was not.

"I learned, Jessie, that life is a gamble. There are no rights and wrongs. We can play the rules or break them. We can meet a soul-mate and marry them, or find many soul-mates and play them. There is no map on the table. You have to know yourself to play Baccarat. Not many do. At your age I thought I was invincible. I wanted to learn, and I wanted to persevere, to travel, to conquer.

However... in amongst the disarray of my desire for power, I found the woman who showed me who I really was."

"Your wife stopped you gambling, Tristan?"

"That's where you are wrong... I stopped me gambling for <u>then</u>... but if you took me to Vegas tomorrow, I would play. Yes... I would play..."

Bridget yelled: "Is this a cruise ship... are we on vacation..?" "Hurry along, Jessie... the clients are not wanting to hear your life story."

Yet again Bridget, who I was so in fear of, had protected me.

"Bridget... I... I... did not deserve what you did for me today... I did let you down... you could have said how bad I was... you are within your rights..."

"Come on now... let's leave the sentimentals for another day... you are the best damn psychic I have... and that's profit... now off you go..."

I learned that day that Bridget and Tristan were my family and we had to protect each other. They had found their way to forgive me, though I had no idea why.

Carina was my first client of the day and she was extremely sullen.

"Almodine for goodness sake, where have you been? I assume it wasn't a world cruise?"

I assumed position as Almodine and smiled meekly.

"How may I help you, Carina? Do you have a direct question I can answer... or perhaps just a general overview of what I see..."

"Cut the blurb Almodine, I am paying good money for this. I want to know about a guy called Rowe... surname Rowe... your initial impression? I don't get a good vibe about him at all... don't <u>like</u> him, don't <u>trust</u> him... mmm... well...?"

It was obvious that Carina knew the answer herself. Carina <u>always</u> knew the answer herself, and I was there merely to mirror her initial reaction.

I took my time. I closed my eyes for a few seconds... I knew Rowe was absolutely fine, but a man to cause her any negativity, but as I opened my eyes I could see Carina's impatience.

"Well, Carina... I feel strongly you should trust your gut instinct. I feel Rowe respects you in the workplace..."

Carina screwed up her face in disbelief.

"Are you kidding me? <u>Respects</u> me? He cannot abide me. No way does he respect me."

I had to salvage the reading as Carina was used to dominating every reading, which made me wonder if I was merely a listening ear.

"Well... Carina... as you know, Rowe is a complex man..."

Carina shook her head. "Enough about Rowe... will the contract come through that I'm expecting... delays... I am so tired of delays... and if you could give me the answers a bit quicker I would appreciate it. This contract is lucrative... and I have worked so..."

I could not believe what I was feeling. I did not sense a contract at all. I could not see it in front of me. Therefore I had to assume Carina was going to be disappointed.

Carina drummed her fingers on the arm rest of the chair. "Don't fret, I have a decent lawyer to deal with the contract, that's not an issue... so when will the contract come through?"

Carina was exhausting, but I sensed whatever the business contract was that she wanted so badly... I would have to word this carefully.

"Almodine, I think it will be in the next ten days... and I am not normally wrong... well what do you see?"

"The thing is Carina... contracts are quite tricky to read sometimes... timing can be difficult around any type of documents."

Carina threw her handbag on the floor in front of my desk. "Look, stop the psychic babble... when?"

"I - I - I think there could be a significant delay... that could be a positive. I mean, as I read it there is fate that plays a hand... if the contract was not meant... then I am sure you would accept that Carina..."

Unfortunately my wording had not gone down very well at all.

"What exactly do you mean, if the contract was not meant... are you saying all the work I have done is on the scrap? I hope you are very wrong.... I have a meeting and this reading has been a let down..."

I tried to backtrack. I did not want Carina to feel cheated in any way. I always felt responsible when I read for clients, perhaps too responsible.

"Remember, Carina... nothing is <u>concrete</u>, readings change daily, or weekly."

Carina looked furious. "If you think I will pay for readings weekly as, hey presto, you might see a contract, you are on a hiding to nothing. Good day to you."

Carina always had her own agenda, but I felt strangely at ease with even her most venomous retorts. It was her inner frustration, not anything personal.

Vented frustration and discontentment was all part of being Almodine.

My next client was like no-one I had ever talked to before. When I read for people... if they were in pain or distress I really wanted to make them feel better... but in an hour it is difficult.

"Can I get your name, please?"

The man was in his late forties and shuffled in his seat, looking visibly uncomfortable.

"Eh... my name is Lawrence. Does it matter if that's a middle name?"

"Lawrence, that is absolutely fine. I just need a name for the records. Please don't worry. Now, how can I help you. Is it a general reading or a specific question?"

It became like a script, and that I was merely providing a staged introduction to my psychic persona.

Lawrence seemed to hesitate. "I would like to see what you pick up around me... but it is a <u>specific</u> question. Can I just ask you <u>out loud</u>?"

I was intrigued, but I sensed that Lawrence was fighting within himself what he should and should not do. Lawrence was a deep thinker, but troubled. I sensed it had taken courage to even walk inside the building.

"Please ask the question, Lawrence?"

"Does Belinda realise what she has done to me? If she does realise, should I go ahead with the procedure I am thinking about? The procedure that will make life so much easier?"

Lawrence could not maintain any kind of eye contact with me.

"I feel, Lawrence, that Belinda has absolutely <u>no idea</u> what she has done to you. Belinda follows her own path and rarely listens to anyone else. This is the issue, she is very headstrong. You realise this..."

Lawrence looked more frantic, his eyes suddenly looking at me, pleading. "Belinda is really a good person... she comes across to you as a good person, doesn't she?"

I closed my eyes. Belinda had little interest in Lawrence. It felt a very faint friendship.

"Belinda does <u>care</u> about you, Lawrence. I do feel that... yet how do I say it... mmm... it's like she is attached to someone else. I sense a ring... a designed ring. It feels like someone else. It feels to me... like she is engaged. Yes, I see the ring..."

Lawrence shook his head, as if in denial.

"She is engaged, just last week... not really sure how it came about. This man... he does not care about her like I do... certainly not in the same way. I was shocked when I heard, really could not take it in..."

I sensed that Belinda had been in a relationship for years with her fiancée, so was very unsure why the confusion.

"I - I - I did not actually <u>know</u> Belinda as such, maybe not in the traditional way. We met in a coffee shop, and we had a good chat. I don't really see that many people day to day... I live on my own you see.

Our friendship just grew organically you might say. I got to know the car she drove and when I saw her parking, which was in the same side street, I would make my own way to the coffee shop."

I was quite taken aback at Lawrence being quite so open with me, especially as it seemed they had no relationship at all, not even acquaintances. They were really strangers, and Lawrence was trying to contrive things.

"She normally has two coffees, the first one is a Cappuccino, which is large, and she eats two croissants with marmalade, or sometimes apricot jam. She usually sits on her own with a newspaper, but she would <u>always</u> speak to me... as I waited for my coffee. So we chatted perhaps two or three minutes... sometimes five minutes. I would like to think average five minutes. I would look at my watch afterwards.

You see, Belinda seems a very nice person... she always takes the time to say good morning, which I think is a good sign isn't it? You can tell <u>a lot</u> about someone how they take the time out of their day even to smile."

I did not want to use the word obsessive, but Lawrence clearly was delusional. I wanted to try and find a positive pathway which would allow him to see past Belinda. I needed to focus... and quickly...

"You know how I mentioned the procedure? I am thinking about some cosmetic procedures... nothing too drastic... just so she notices me... that's important, isn't it? Looking your best self is really important. It's all energy, isn't it? If I look good on the <u>outside</u>, she may take a bigger chance at looking at me on the inside. That's my plan. I have the pictures.

I got a pay-out for stress in the workplace, and so I looked into it... got the brochures... if I looked younger Belinda would spend more time noticing me. I just want to look slightly different."

This reading was draining. It was apparent I was seeing a man refusing to accept the truth.

"Can I ask how you actually found out Belinda was engaged?"

"Oh... she showed the ring to one of the women who work at the coffee shop as they noticed it sparkling I suppose. I could have bought Belinda a much more expensive diamond ring if she wanted it... that would have been no issue. I have been very, very confused since I found out. You think everything is going along steady, and then you realise that it's being taken away."

"Belinda wasn't really yours in the first place though, was she? She was being well-mannered but she had not done anything with negative intention. She was not trying to fool you as such... she did not know you at all. I'm sorry, Lawrence, but you need to move on. You really need to try."

"I have seen the man she is supposedly engaged to... only the once mind... they were in the coffee shop, not holding hands or anything. Don't you think that tells you something? They were not holding hands so they must be over?"

"Lawrence, I feel you see so little of Belinda, it is really impossible to judge. I understand... it is what you <u>think</u> you want. It is a <u>glimpse</u> of something you would like, but I am afraid it is not <u>real</u>."

"I - I do not believe what you are saying. You are probably a <u>fake</u>... in it for the money to buy yourself a fancy car to drive. You don't realise... <u>listen</u> to anyone properly do you? You just wanted to make me think I was lying to myself when I wasn't. It gives you some sense of being someone you are not. You are <u>nothing</u> lady. A nobody. Belinda is everything you would love to be. Her face is like porcelain, perfect. She has the most perfect handwriting. I have seen her write in a notebook. Perfect. Perfect, <u>everything</u>."

I remembered Tristan mention the emergency button on the desk, and I pressed it three times for good measure. Within seconds Tristan appeared.

"So sorry, Almodine, we will have to give you a break now... other clients are waiting and your schedule is full today. Apologies, sir, let me take your coat."

"I am surprised you are busy..." snarled Lawrence. "I bet you are not even a mother, are you? If you ever were you would be a lousy one... you have not broken me... no way... Belinda <u>loves</u> me, and I love <u>her</u> unconditionally... you are not even important enough to hate..."

Tristan picked up Lawrence's belongings. "Let's leave now sir... it's easier that way."

Lawrence stared at me straight in the face.

"I meant every single word I said, Lousy Mother."

That phrase... lousy mother, resonated in my head and I could hear it over and over as I tried to think it was meaningless. I hoped this was not a spiritual test, and I had failed miserably.

Tristan brought me a cup of tea. "Some people don't want to be helped. Talking to you is just like waiting at a bus stop, as they want anonymity. They don't want to show weakness. Today was not personal. You could have been anyone. You were just there at the time... do you understand? You were just a bystander?"

I did understand, even though I did not want to. It was best not to think too hard, and let the pain of others wash all over you.

Chapter Twenty-Three

Tristan smiled: "We have our regular... Jeanne... do you have time to see her? I feel for her... every Thursday afternoon... same time for the last few years... bless her."

"Of course I'll see her... send her in..."

Jeanne walked in tentatively. "Oh, you're back! I really missed you... things have been difficult... and as you know... I've got no-one really to talk to at home. It's difficult... when you feel you are living a lie."

Jeanne looked desperately tired with her drawn face, and accentuated lines around her eyes and mouth. She looked emotionally drained.

"Take a seat, Jeanne... would you like a cup of tea... fruit juice?"

"Oh Almodine... I'm fine thank you... just desperate to see what you pick up."

I remembered Jeanne had been seeing a married man for over twenty years, and it was going nowhere.

"Just take some deep breaths and relax, Jeanne... let's see what I pick up."

As I connected I could sense that the scenario had become distinctly more complicated. The man that Jeanne was having the affair with for all these years, had not only his wife but another woman around him... it was a new energy... it had been going on for several weeks. There was no way I could tell Jeanne.

"Is everything alright, Almodine? You have gone a bit pale... <u>you can</u> tell me anything you see."

I felt terrible... like a back-street charlatan, but Jeanne was simply not strong enough for the truth.

"I - I - I sense communication lines may go down, but then improve again... so try not to worry. The man you have been seeing has been quiet of late, and when he does speak to you... it is like you don't know him... he is agitated... angry with you all the time. It <u>will</u> get better. I see that..."

"You are right, Almodine, I felt I could do nothing right with him... it's like I merged in with the wallpaper. I wasn't always like this you know... weak... pathetic. I used to be free-spirited before I got married... always fun to be around... What's happened to me? I would not want to be with me... my messy hair... my drabness. My husband gives me an allowance you see... you cannot overspend... or look in the mirror too much. It's pointless. I'd like to break away from being a mistress, a whore, a wife, a nobody. I didn't do college... I thought I knew better you see. I wanted to run away, get married and have my own house, my own cooker to clean, my own curtains... now it's all I've got. The cooker, the curtains."

"Jeanne... you have the <u>power</u> to change things... you know you have... Besides, the man you are seeing <u>does</u> love you... in his own way. He is just the type of man who runs to his cave... the emotional shutdown... it is who he is.

I actually see education around you, Jeanne... I see you gong to university... something you have always wanted to do. You will <u>succeed</u>. I see you in the gown... with your scroll... and I can hear all the applause Jeanne... You will succeed."

Jeanne was beaming. She suddenly looked twenty years younger.

"You really see it? I have always wanted to make something of myself. Who would have thought it... someone like me... going to university... That's all I needed today... someone who <u>believed</u> in me..."

Jeanne walked away from me a different woman, her shoulders pulled back... taller. She had belief. I don't believe I lied. I believe I threw her a lifeline she so desperately needed.

Tristan waved... "Well, another day, another dollar. You must be over the moon about seeing your boy. You are being given a second chance. Grab it with both hands! Be who you are. Show the world the <u>real</u> Jessie and it will light your path."

Tristan never doubted me, nor did Bridget. I had never had that unfailing support before.

"Do you ever get afraid Tristan? You don't seem afraid of anything."

"Jessie... do not be fooled. I have had my share of fear. I am no warrior. I am just an old man with plenty of optimism. You see, just like you... I need this job. It means I am not just sitting at home in my little apartment wondering how to take my coffee. I don't want to be that old guy circling the grocery store for company. Who wants that?

I might just be on reception here. I might not have any visible gifts like yourself. If I open the door, take someone's name... maybe cup of tea... some pleasantries... then who knows... maybe I have made a difference. We all need to make a small difference.

So at night... I can look at the stars and think: Tristan, you did a little bit of good today."

Tristan had the most amazing energy. To me he did not appear like an old man at all. He was vibrant, and warm. He put his trust in me.

"Tristan... so you know, you have more than a visible gift. You are a friend to me, and so many people... what greater gift is that?"

"You get yourself home now Jessie... before my head cannot fit through the door.

Oh... and I am so happy you are finally going to see your boy. Don't push everyone away because you are frightened Jessie. Bridget understands more than anyone. See past the obvious Jessie, and you will do alright."

I smiled at Tristan. I do already. I always have, and always will.

Chapter Twenty-Four

I was pleased with how the day had gone. I felt elated that I would have money to treat Noah, and it would be no struggle. I had pay from Bridget, and from Golda, though I would have to be cleaning into the night... as Edward, the unwelcome visitor, was watching my every move.

I walked past my favourite little artisan bakery on the walk to Golda's. I liked to stare at the pastries. Noah used to love pain au chocolat warm, and a cup of warm milk.

I thought it may be a good idea to have a little box of cakes... maybe cupcakes and with Noah's name on... sort of a surprise... all wrapped in a fancy box.

I could buy a new toy... and maybe a new anorak... For once I had all the money to spend on Noah... yes, Noah to spend it on.

"Hey Jessie... were you going to walk away from me! How are you?"

I turned around, and to my dismay it was tousle-haired Matty, alone.

"Hey... how are tricks?"

This was really not the time I wanted to see, Matty. I was already half an hour late to make Golda's dinner.

"You... you... look awkward... like you don't want to see me. This isn't the Jessie I know and <u>love</u>. Let's go for a gin... come on... you are always so highly strung. Try and be fun."

"Matty, I don't need any fun. I'm holding down two jobs. I just want calm, and to get on with things."

Matty had obviously been drinking. His eyes looked bleary, and his ruddy complexion aged him. Matty looked more unkempt than I had seen him for a long time.

"You have changed Jessie. The <u>old</u> Jessie would have drunk gin with me at the drop of a hat and never questioned anything. The <u>old</u> Jessie would have sat having coffee in Delaney's and having a sing song. The <u>old</u> Jessie would have done <u>anything</u> for me."

It was shocking to me that Matty suddenly looked pathetic. He looked weak, and somebody that I hardly knew.

"Do anything for you? You mean sleep with you in a hotel where everyone knows your name, and give me the most run-down apartment next to a brothel. You are <u>all</u> heart Matty. What can I say?"

It was then without warning that Matty turned to me and grabbed my arm, twisting my right wrist.

"You should be grateful. You had <u>nothing</u> before you met me. <u>Nothing</u>. You even got your kid taken away. Why? Because you are a head case. Complete and utter head case. Look at yourself in the mirror. Who else would have wanted to sleep with you in a hotel, eh? Come on... no-one in their right mind... with cutting marks all over your arms and legs. Head case, through and through.

I am going to put you up against that wall over there and teach you a lesson."

Matty was physically stronger than I remembered, as he pulled me against my will.

"Shut your mouth, or I will be the one with the blade doing the cutting... got it?"

At the time of being attacked in Matty's apartment I was silent. This time I could not be silent. I screamed. It was instinct. It was me fighting to go home to Golda, for everything I had worked for so far.

Everything after that was a blur, greyness, noise, Matty's watch smashing on the pavement and a man smelling of strong woody cologne dressed in an immaculate pin-stripe suit yelling: "Get your hands off her..."

I slowly turned my face which had been tucked into my chest to hide my shame at even having spoken to Matty.

To my horror, the man with the stench of cologne was Edward. I could not believe it. How was I going to salvage this.

Matty shrugged his shoulders. "Look man, it's all a bit of a misunderstanding. I've had a drink or two... it's not what it looked like. It was play fighting, banter. Man to man, we've all been there... pretty girl out on her own... you know..."

Edward snarled at Matty, "Get the hell out of here... and leave her alone. She <u>works</u> for me. She is not your property. She is <u>mine</u>. You infringe on what belongs to me... and there will be consequences that might be difficult for you, <u>very</u> difficult."

Matty nodded his head in an exaggerated fashion, and ran quicker to save himself, not me.

Edward had a driver, and I sat in the back of the car, <u>compliant</u>. The luxurious seats felt uncomfortable. I felt suddenly smaller than the driver's ashtray.

Edward smirked. "Who was he? Stay away from bar brawl in the street or you will be sacked, plain and simple. You don't understand fancy language, so I'll keep it to the bare bones. You may think my mother is in charge, but it's me. It always has been. I'm in charge of her finances, everything. Don't over think anything, and do as you're told and we will get along just fine."

The drive to Golda's seemed endless. I stared straight ahead. I did not turn to look at Edward once. I felt sorry for Golda. I think she knew deep down Edward was a second rate opportunist with no interest in his mother. Golda lived in a gilded cage that I was no part of. I stood on the outside, polishing the gold. It was the safest place to be.

Chapter Twenty-Five

Edward acted out of character, and kept quiet about what he saw in the street. I knew he was not protecting me, he was protecting himself.

Working with Bridget had taught me an important lesson: be honest with yourself, act with integrity, for whatever the response you have tried.

I knew that Edward wanted to control me and his mother. The fact that I had withheld the truth about having a son would make Golda question my identity, and if I was worthy to clean her home.

"Golda, I must speak to you now, it is very important. It is a private matter."

Golda was playing patience at her small side table and looked bemused.

"A private matter... you wish to borrow money? How much?"

"No Golda... I'm sorry, it's not money. You misunderstand. It's a more... delicate matter."

Edward glared at me from the doorway.

"I cannot speak about this in front of Edward, as you hired me. It is imperative I speak to you."

Edward defiantly walked towards his mother.

"I will deal with any issues. I'm in charge here. You cannot deal with stress, mother."

Golda snapped. "Edward, I have had enough of your impertinence. Now, please leave us alone for a private conversation. Immediately... thank you."

Edward always had the ability to look sullen, even when he was not.

"Golda... I am afraid I have lied to you... well not exactly lied, just withheld the truth. I am not proud of myself, I just needed a proper chance. I am needing this job to finance getting my son, Noah... he is in care... I couldn't cope. I did try, but when the electricity kept cutting off and taking Noah to school got harder... you know everything costs money these days... I did try, honest I did.

I didn't have anywhere to go. I'll pack my bag, and if it's alright with you, I will make dinner, and do all the cleaning that's required. I won't require payment of course. I just wanted to apologise. I'm not a bad person, really I'm not."

Golda sat up with a jolt and gave no visible reaction to my words.

"Where is the father?"

I had been honest this far, so I was compelled to continue.

"He is married. I thought he was different, you know, important. It was all a mirage. I was stupid, really, really stupid. I was not brought up that way, and when everyone found out about Noah I was thrown out.

I was lucky. I got a little job making sandwiches in a little café, and there was a small apartment above the shop. I lived there. It was small, but it was warm. Sadly, it was a family business and the grandparents wanted to retire. I was given notice, but I had to leave two weeks before Noah was born.

I was in labour in the homeless shelter. I wore a big coat you see, it hid my tummy... meant I was able to work... get the money for a bed and breakfast.

I remember the day Noah was born... the midwife was called Autumn. She said: "We will get you both clean and ready for your visitors."

Me and Noah, we lay there ourselves. There were no visitors.

It was funny because from the hospital window all the other mothers had all these people chattering excitedly. I thought, I wonder what it would be like... you know, to have someone there.

I didn't think long about it. I just looked at Noah, and thought: "We are together, and I won't let you down."

My son was taken away from me, as I was seen as not in the best interest for Noah, whatever that means. If I save up my money, I will be able to get the best lawyer... you know one that will actually care."

123

Golda bowed her head, "I'm hungry... off you go and get dinner ready..."

"Shall I pack my bag afterwards and leave. My room is tidy... I promise you."

"There will be no time for you to leave as you have a parquet flooring to clean, and the silver to polish, plenty to do."

Golda did not give me any emotion, only errands and for that I was grateful.

"My tea is stone cold Jessie... your mind is somewhere else. There is no point in working for me if you are all over the place. Do you understand?"

"Golda... I see my son this weekend... it has been so long. I - I don't know if he will... still love me. How will I know? What will I do if he has moved his feelings to a new mother?"

Golda beckoned me over to the gold brocade fancy looking armchair that she never sat on.

"Sit. Put the silver cutlery down. You probably think I have it all, don't you?"

I was quiet. I was not misguided enough to say anything.

"You probably think I have it all don't you... after all you are just a young girl? I have this grandiose house...it's all I ever wanted. My husband looked after me you see. I didn't have to see or look at anything to do with money. He was the investor, the banker, the visionary. I... I just had to look beautiful. As I got older... it was harder... it's harder to look in the mirror. One day you may be just like me..."

As I looked at Golda almost feeling sorry for herself with her extensive wealth, I could not see me ever being like her, not now, nor in the future.

"You see... it's all very well being independent but you need a <u>husband</u>, a <u>protector</u>, someone to take care of you. Independence is over-rated in my opinion."

"Golda, I need to stand on my own two feet. A husband may be good for some people, but not for me. I speak with wide eyes. Husbands can let you down, they come and go. If they do all the investments and banking, what as a woman do you actually gain from that? Where does it place you in life? It places you in the garbage bin... no good to anyone. I won't let any man <u>destroy</u> my ability to think for myself... not now, <u>not ever</u>."

Golda looked stunned, but I wasn't sorry.

I wasn't sorry at all.

Chapter Twenty-Six

I was stronger than Golda, Edward or any of their entourage. I felt that I was meant to live in that cold, unimaginative, cobweb of a house to see what I didn't want, and sometimes that's important.

Just as I made my way to the hallway, Edward was sitting on the tiled floor shuffling a pack of cards.

"Is everything alright, Edward? Do you need anything before morning?"

Edward looked sullen. "Do I <u>look</u> like I need anything as I sit here alone? What a mindless thing to say... my mother thinks you are little Miss Perfect, but I think I know people. You don't succeed in business without knowing people. I think you hold a lot of dark secrets dear to you... a lot.

This place... it's your hiding place. A sanctuary. Yet I know this... everything catches up with you in the end."

Edward was the master of talking in riddles. It made him feel important. I was in no mood to listen to his venom, but stood politely.

"Why the hell are you here? You know what my mother is... she can do nothing for herself. She probably pays you a pittance."

"This isn't about what your mother <u>cannot</u> do, this is about me helping, that is all."

Edward laughed out loud, and the echo of his laughter was magnified against the cold walls.

"You haven't got anywhere to go, have you? No-one actually wants you. Did your parents get disappointed with you... did they ask you to close the door quietly when you left. Did they ask you never to come back?"

Edward continued laughing so loudly I wanted to cover my ears.

"Stop Edward, please stop..."

"The truth is, little Jessie, you whored yourself to a man who had a wife and you were a laughing stock. You had a kid, and nobody wanted either of you. Which means you are stuck. It means you are stuck in this prison of a place and I am in charge here, not my mother."

I didn't know what happened, but within minutes I had run to Edward, and the cards were strewn all over the sterile tiles.

My hand was at Edward's jaw. "Shut up, do you hear me? Shut up. Don't you ever speak to me that way. You don't own me. Nobody owns me. I am in charge of my own life. I can walk out of here tomorrow, and never look back.

Put me up against a wall Edward, kick me until my head hurts. Rape me, until I cannot feel. Go on. I am standing here. I am your punch bag. Go on..."

Edward bowed his head and scrambled to pick up each card tentatively off the floor.

"I hate you Edward, and I don't hate anyone... not enough that's important. I don't even hate the men that attacked me. They are not in my head space. They do not matter. I didn't feel it. I closed my eyes, and it didn't hurt. Besides, anything that is repeated doesn't hurt. Not that you care.

I could hit you fifty times and you could have me charged with being a lunatic. Do you know, maybe I'm a lunatic... working here for a loser like you who does not even love his fiancée, and she does not love him."

Edward lifted his head and stared at me. "What do you mean, she doesn't love me..?"

"She hates your guts, Edward. You know that all that glitters is not gold. You can buy and sell me. You always could, but I wouldn't spit on the ground you walk on..."

I slumped to the floor, exhausted. It was the first time I had ever talked about the attack, and I was mortified that Edward was the one to hear my story.

It was like calmness after an electrical storm. Edward and I sat opposite each other in silence, not knowing what to say.

Golda's heeled shoes clicked, like I was being led to the gallows.

"Stand up Jessie Lindemann. Who do you think you are, young miss, talking to my son like that? It is unacceptable under my roof, and I will not tolerate it. Your wages will be deducted, one day's wage will be removed for utter insolence.

Do you understand, Jessie Lindemann, for if you do not understand then you should pack your bags now."

"I do understand, Golda..."

"For the next week you will not join me in the drawing room, and will bring food to me in silence. If I find dust or filth anywhere, both Edward and I will dock your wages further. The penny will drop for you, Jessie Lindemann, that your fiery spirit will mean that you succeed at nothing..."

Golda walked slowly up to my face.

"Pretty girl with long hair... wouldn't it be a shame if your long hair was cut short. I have the power to do that you know. In fact... I'll strike you a deal. I will cut your hair short and will not dock your wages at all. Which do you prefer... hair short or pennies in gold? You have the power to decide."

Edward stood up: "Leave the girl alone, mother... she doesn't deserve it. I pushed her around and she stood up for herself. It was me, not her. Leave her be."

"Be careful, Edward... I know plenty about you, so do not forget that."

"Like I say, mother... the girl hasn't asked for any of this. She does her job fine, she deserves to be paid."

I could not believe Edward was actually standing up for me.

Golda shrugged her shoulders and sidled away, no doubt to drink herself to sleep.

Edward looked ashamed. "It sounds like you have been through it... it wasn't personal... I just get angry and everything erupts inside of me. I then realise I've gone too far. It's not an excuse. I think I should probably be less of someone that you hate, and more of someone that you hate less. We have to exist of sorts here."

I felt bad at what I had said to Edward. "I - I - didn't mean about your fiancée. I was just angry. I - didn't see anything. I was angry and didn't think."

"You meant it alright. I could see it in your eyes. I admire honesty. It's a good trait. Don't lose that."

I leaned to pick up the remaining playing cards off the floor and handed them tentatively to Edward.

"You need to make your own decisions Edward."

"I know that... all the past... my mistakes... they seem to follow me."

I smiled. "I know that more than most. I abandoned my son, so you were right, I did run away and I'm still running."

"You abandoned him? You mean like gave him away to a relative?" Edward was being uncharacteristically empathetic.

"There was no-one to help, just me. They didn't give me a choice. I - I - had no choice. I need this job here. I need to pay my way, get a good lawyer. I need to find a way forward."

Edward looked at me anxiously.

"Where are your family?"

I wanted to walk away from this conversation. I wanted to walk really badly.

"My mother re-married. My step-father didn't want me around, you know the deal. He said there would be no college, or things that I didn't need. He told my mother I didn't need lunch money for school, and he told my mother to teach me to be independent. My mother changed. I didn't recognise her. She travelled the world with him on cruise ships, Las Vegas, everywhere to be seen."

"Did you go with them around the world?"

"No. I stayed at home, except it wasn't home. It was just a shell, and I didn't belong there. A week after they returned home my bag was packed and I ran away, aged sixteen."

"So they found you... they brought you home, right?"

"Wrong... there were no posters or signs in windows. My mother let me go."

Edward was quiet. "I'm sorry... what's your name again...?"

I was too tired to be angry at Edward. He had only just noticed I actually existed.

"It's Jessie... Jessie Lindemann."

Edward reached out his hand. "Pleased to meet you, Jessie Lindemann. I genuinely wish you well."

I could hardly stay awake. It had been a long day.

"Can I get you anything else, Edward. I have to be up early... would it be alright...?"

Edward looked flustered. "Of course... yes... I mean... goodnight."

I didn't really know Edward any better that night. I didn't know what to make of him at all.

Chapter Twenty-Seven

Breakfast was quiet. There was no sign of Edward, which made me breathe easier. Golda, however, was unpleasantly critical, as expected.

"My son, Edward, is getting married in a marquee made of glass. The floral arrangements on each table absolutely stunning."

I wasn't listening. I just wanted to clear the breakfast dishes and be at Bridget's on time. I wanted Bridget to be able to trust me, especially as Noah would be visiting me at her house. I would be on lighthouse watch. I would be on display for everyone to see. I actually could not quite absorb that I would see Noah after all this time. I was elated, but my heart was filled with fear.

I tidied up the kitchen quickly, but as I turned around to leave Edward was standing in the doorway.

"Someone is in a rush... what is the hurry.. ?"

Edward or Golda had no idea I worked with Bridget and that was the way it would have to be.

"So... what is your other occupation, Jessie... do you clean another house?"

I didn't want to tell la lie, but sometimes there is no choice.

"I do clean a few houses... so if you don't mind, I'll be on my way."

Edward looked understanding. "Of course, off you go... Oh, I meant to say, my fiancée is going to have dinner this evening at ours. I was thinking, langoustine, maybe a terrine to start... and I am thinking a lemon sorbet, and perhaps a chocolate parfait. I take it that won't be a problem for you..."

I wanted to yell out loud as it would mean I could not afford to take any late extra readings at Bridget's. Edward was infringing on my ability to earn. This was my big week, before Noah was visiting. I needed money in my pocket, and I needed everything perfect.

"Oh, and dinner for seven, no later..."

"Yes, Edward... seven will be fine."

"I want everything to be perfect for Fleur, do you understand?"

"Yes, I do. It will be perfect."

As I grabbed my coat, I was unaware that Edward was whispering to his driver.

"This week you have a job to do. I want that girl followed, ask your friend, Eduardo... he is sharp... quick-witted. I think the girl lies so much she does not know who she actually is."

The driver looked quiet. "She looks about the same age as my daughter. She seems harmless enough... she is always very pleasant. She always says good morning, and asks how I am... I have never seen any trouble. None at all."

"I pay you to be my driver. I <u>do not</u> pay you to be a Psychologist. It was merely a fact. Get Eduardo to follow her. Thieves and criminals act plausible. They act pleasant. I want every single snippet of information on that woman. I think she is a fraud, and I can smell a fraud from a thousand paces."

The drive shook his head. "I think she is trying to pay her way is all, sir..."

Edward looked confused. "Pay her way for what?"

"Pay bills, sir."

"Ask Eduardo... and I will get the agency onto it... her time is extremely limited with free lodgings and board..."

The driver turned his head.

"If you don't mind, sir, she is up at the crack of dawn cooking, cleaning and fetching deliveries. She insists on walking with all the bags. She is incredibly independent..."

"Another sign of a liar. Independence."

"How long have you been a driver for my mother?"

The driver smiled: "Twelve years, and never missed a day."

"Well make sure you find every bit of dirt on Jessie Lindemann, and your family will receive financial reward. Substantial financial reward.

"Yes sir, I understand."

I walked to Bridget's hurriedly. I liked to talk to Tristan before the start of the day.

I walked past the same church standing on a hill. I felt drawn to go and light a candle, just for a little while.

I felt safe in that church. The stained glass windows that shone golden shards of light on my face. The incense smell of old hopes and wishes.

I walked reverently to the small altar, and kneeled for a few minutes.

"I pray for Noah. I pray for answers. I hope that Bridget acts like she respects me when the Social Worker sees me. I - I pray that Noah does not run away from me when he sees me after all this time. He may run away. He may hate me. He may think I abandoned him for my own gain."

I could hear footsteps. It was time to leave.

A Priest, young, with piercing bluey grey eyes, smiled at me.

"Can I help you in any way? Would you like a mass said for someone?"

"No, Father, I am not <u>good</u> enough to get a mass said... you see it would be for me... for guidance... and my son..."

"On the contrary, I can say a mass... perhaps you would like to share what is troubling you..."

"No, Father... I am afraid I can't... it's not that simple..."

"Father David... if you need to talk to someone who will listen..."

I was taken aback. "I will try to attend church more often..."

"I think you carry emotional burdens for someone so young. As I say, I do not judge."

I felt a strange sense of calm as I walked to Bridget's that morning. This would be a tougher week than I had ever known, or could ever imagine.

Chapter Twenty-Eight

Bridget greeted me as I arrived. "I'd like to see you in my office please, hurry along..."

I was confused. Obviously one of my clients had complained about a reading, which was not unusual.

"I want you to be fully prepared for this week-end, Jessie. I will have my living room pristine... books... games... child-friendly. This Social Worker will be eagle-eyed. She will be looking for every little detail. We need to be prepared.

I will have lots of healthy foods in the fridge, and we will show this woman you have stability for Noah... a luxurious place to live."

I felt confused, I felt a sinking feeling in my stomach as, really, we were lying to the Social Worker. The fact that I, allegedly, lived in this grandiose house of Bridget's was a bare-faced lie. Even more worrying, Noah was not used to living in a big house. He was used to following me from place to place in lots of run down apartments.

This was going to be a change, a big change.

"You don't look very happy, Jessie. What's wrong?"

I didn't want to talk to Bridget. I wanted to keep my emotions to myself.

"It's nothing to worry about, being scared. It's absolutely fine to be afraid of the things we cannot see. It's the thought of what may happen that is worse than what actually may take place. You <u>can</u> get through this Jessie..."

"Do you think? Do you really believe they are going to side with a young girl in board and lodgings who gave birth in a homeless shelter, turfed out by her parents. A kid who would not name the father on the birth certificate? You have far more faith than me, Bridget... I think the Social Worker is going to hang me out to dry. The Psychologist, Social worker and Noah's school.

It's like it's all closing in. The ceiling is coming down on top of my head. There is no escape.

If I was wealthy, then yes. If I had affluent parents, status, then yes, I could do what the hell I wanted.

However, if you are a <u>nobody</u> there is no lifeline. You are left to wonder the where and the when..."

Bridget looked serious, and held my gaze.

"<u>Do not</u> give up. You <u>must</u> keep going. Do not let anyone else say what you should do, or believe. Noah is your son. Now is not the time to give up."

I felt helpless. I felt like every day this week was a stepping stone to the day I would be on show to the world.

"Busy day for you, Jessie... I've booked in extra readings to take your mind off things. You need work, more than ever."

Tristan arrived with a cup of tea.

"I got you a little jam biscuit since this is a special week for you..."

"Thank you, Tristan... I appreciate that, but it's just an ordinary week for me..."

Tristan looked shocked. "Oh... I have a present for your Noah downstairs. Just wait till you see it... a real treat. His little eyes will light up... he has probably missed you so much he is going to run to you... and everything is going to be just as it was before..."

I didn't want to hear Tristan talking about Noah and I. It didn't feel right. I didn't know what to <u>say</u> or what to think.

Bridget looked agitated. "A word outside please, Tristan love... <u>now</u>."

I sat gazing at my cup of tea, and wrapped the biscuit in a napkin for later. "Tristan, Jessie is not coping at all. I'm worried about her. It's alright that we bring the little boy to my place that's like a show home... but if Jessie is going to go into self-destruct mode... where is this going to leave her?"

Tristan shook his head. "She has too much on her plate... those young shoulders with a heavy heart. She needs more company... she is lonely, the girl..."

Bridget rolled her eyes. "We don't need the amateur psychology... you need to take her for a coffee or a dinner after work today... boost her confidence..."

"Bridget, behave yourself... I am an <u>old man</u>... what can I offer...? Nothing."

Bridget put her arm around Tristan's shoulders. "On the contrary, you can offer her friendship... unconditional friendship. That is <u>all</u> she needs right now..."

"Bridget, what about the present for Noah. What do you want me to do... put it in the store cupboard?"

"Tristan, leave the present till Friday. It's all too much for her right now. She is like an emotional volcano, waiting to erupt."

Chapter Twenty-Nine

Tristan greeted me gently with my first client of the day.

"It's Felina with a twenty minute reading for you..."

"So this is Almodine... I have heard you are good. How do you read... Pendulum? Gypsy cards? Runes?"

I could tell within seconds Felina needed boundaries. She needed order, structure in her life. She wanted to take control of the reading, and I was not going to allow it.

"Please relax Felina. My name is Almodine, should you wish another reading..."

Felina snapped: "The old guy downstairs told me who you were... I'm paying good money for this, so enlighten me... when am I going to meet a new woman?"

I listened while Felina again was determined to take control of the reading.

"I have had a string of hopeless cases... you know, women who have lousy jobs and cannot look after themselves. As you can see, I am successful. I have several properties, a nice car... and I travel extensively..."

I felt Felina needed me to say absolutely nothing. She felt the need to sell herself, and I had to try to maintain concentration.

"I want a woman with intelligence. She has to handle me, my parrot Antonio and my tropical fish."

I listened intently, though the conversation was desperately mundane.

"I want the woman to be tall... perhaps Nordic... you know... sophisticated... ice-grey eyes, no freckles, good taste in clothes. She should be a size six or eight no more. I would not tolerate any more than that. She must take care of herself. She must have an understanding of my job... the pressure I am under all of the time. She cannot be too over the top energy wise, she has to perhaps be prepared to fade into the background. She must have an enigmatic personality... So, Almodine, when do you see all this happening?"

I was stunned. Felina really believed she would meet a woman with all of those attributes. Felina was delusional, and I had to salvage this reading where Felina was running the show, and I had to almost read a script that she wanted to hear, to her specification.

"So... let me connect... I need to close my eyes...tune into your energy."

Felina stood up in a range. "You have said nothing in this reading. I want a refund... it's ridiculous."

"But... Felina... I haven't actually started the reading yet..."

"I'm done. You are not quick enough to match my energy. You do not interest me..."

It was over five minutes so Felina would not get a refund, yet I was relieved. I might only have a fraction of the reading price, but I would be less drained.

Tristan returned quickly: "Don't worry about Felina, it's not personal. She has been blocked from using the Psychics before. She likes to get free readings. Bridget knows her game. I have another client for you. His name is Charlie. Shall I send him through?"

"Of course, thank you Tristan..."

I blocked out the energy of the previous reading with Felina, as that was necessary. Her demanding nature was so toxic

"Hello Charlie, please take a seat. My name is Almodine, and I am a Psychic/Medium."

I could tell Charlie was very nervous, and that it had taken him an immense sense of courage to talk to me.

"So tell me Charlie... is there something specific I can help you with?"

Charlie's hands trembled. "It's all a bit embarrassing. I am not a young man... I don't know how to say it... it's all a bit difficult."

I could sense Charlie's discomfort, and wanted him to feel he was in a safe place.

"Is it a relationship question Charlie... a love issue?"

"Yes it is. I have been on my own for a long time now... and I met this lady... you know when I was out walking. She has a little dog... a scruffy terrier... full of life it is. We got talking... it was a sunny day you see... and I introduced myself. I had seen her lots of times before but we had never spoken. I said it was a lovely day for a walk, and she agreed. Her name is Fran. I don't know much about her, only that she has the most beautiful eyes, and gorgeous silver hair that is plaited down her back. She wears lovely jewellery... an unusual amethyst brooch... you know, Celtic design.

The thing is... I don't want to make a fool of myself. A man of my years. I'd like to take her maybe for coffee or a lunch... would that be acceptable? Or should I just accept that this ship has sailed... and be prepared to walk away. What do you think I should do?"

I could sense illness around Fran. I could see her struggling to walk at night. I also knew how much this connection had meant to Charlie. He was lonely, isolated, there was nothing else to fill his life.

I closed my eyes, and asked Spirit for help.

"Talk to her. Reach out and say, hello Fran, you look lovely today... why don't we go for lunch..? I believe she will grab the opportunity, Charlie..."

I felt empowered. I felt I had said exactly the right thing. Charlie's face lit up.

"You really feel that? You really feel Fran will agree to spend some time with me?"

Charlie's shoulders had relaxed. He was at ease. "When will I see Fran again, Almodine? When do you think... so I can prepare... you know shave properly..."

I smiled. "You should prepare to see her every day Charlie. This is your time to shine.

You are not an old man. You are young in heart, in mind. You can do this."

"You see, not many people believe in me anymore. My grown up son and his wife think I should be in sheltered housing. They want me to sell my home, you know, it means if I have a fall there is assistance. The perils of getting old."

I could see Charlie just wanted someone outside the family to talk to.

"You have to grab opportunities Charlie you and Fran could be great companions, I do see that."

"You do?"

"Of course I do... If you have to go to sheltered housing it will be on your own terms, because it is what you truly believe is right. Your son is led by his wife I believe."

"Do you see perhaps <u>soon</u> that Fran and I might go to dinner? I just want it to happen... the thought... it has given me a new lease of life. I believe you have changed my life today young lady."

I was stunned. Charlie looked like a playful young puppy.

"Thank you with all my heart. You are a lovely person, and I am so happy to have met you."

Charlie extended his hand, and his warmth energised me.

Sometimes you would see clients each week, but I would never again see Charlie.

I sensed that he and Fran <u>did</u> meet, talk and go for lunch. I also sensed that his son rarely visited, so sheltered housing would be the only option.

What made me happiest was that some clients really touch your life, and make you feel a better version of yourself.

I really wanted to see Charlie with his beaming smile again, but sadly I never did.

Chapter Thirty

Tristan looked really tired today, almost ashen faced.

"I wondered if we might get a drink at the Jazz bar after work. It's important that you get some time just to be Jessie... don't you think?"

"You are right, Tristan... maybe I have forgotten who Jessie <u>actually</u> is?"

"Do you want the good news or the bad news, Jessie?"

"It's a tough client, isn't it?"

"Well... it's a forty minute reading with Felina again. She <u>seems</u> apologetic... not sure how long that will last though..."

"I will prepare myself... thank you Tristan. I need to hear some great music... looking forward to later."

Felina walked in sheepishly. "Hello, Almodine, we seemed to get off on the wrong foot..."

Felina was completely backtracking. It was clear none of the other Psychics wanted to talk to her. I thought of my wage, every single note packed into the brown envelope. This was my lifeline, and I was not going to lose that for anything.

"Please take a seat, Felina. How can I help?"

Felina looked awkward, almost regretful.

"I don't come across well sometimes. I say the wrong things. I can be misunderstood."

I tried to put Felina at her ease, and sat at a diagonal at my desk.

"I think being misunderstood happens to us all. I believe that it's just human nature..."

Felina put her handbag on the floor and looked at me intently. "Why do you do this work, I wonder? You seem an intelligent girl, you could work in the city, you seem razor sharp. Why would you work with awkward people like me?"

Felina was warming to me, surprisingly. She was not the confident, brash woman who tried to control me earlier.

"Felina, people who do this type of work are called to do this. It's destined. You do not choose it. I accept this is what I have been given and I do my level best to help people. I try, that's what's important. I read what I see, and I am honest. I am sure you understand honesty is not always popular. It can drive people away.

Felina seemed to be genuinely listening.

"You don't think I will meet a woman to settle down with, do you Almodine?"

I paused... for at this moment I could not see it, but I sensed it was a year's time.

"I believe you need to work from within, Felina, and love yourself. The woman who is your soul mate will love you unconditionally, and love your vibrant energy. She will love you for who you are, Felina. That's what's important."

Felina looked downcast. "How do I work on myself? I have everything, more than one house, cars, more acquaintances than dresses. I have it all."

"Felina, you just need some simplicity in your life. You need someone to hold your hand, go to a desolate beach and stand on craggy rocks while looking at the sea. You need to feel secure. You need to feel safe."

Felina smiled: "Thank you. You are right." She paused. "I got a free reading from you before. I owe you money for your time previously..."

Felina placed money on my desk. I pushed it back.

"I cannot accept that, it was a previous reading. Work on loving yourself again, Felina, and everything will fall into place. You will have a long-term partner who will never betray you. I hope that helps today."

There was no more to tell Felina, and I was not going to waste her time.

"Thank you, Almodine, I'll see you soon... and if you ever want to meet for lunch... we could..."

"I cannot meet clients, Felina, unwritten rules of my work I'm afraid..."

"I understand. I do know a <u>lot</u> of people and you never know... here is my business card, should you need to contact me..."

I took the business card, as everything is given for a reason.

Tristan knocked on the door, unbelievably it was the end of the day. It had been an empowering day.

Tristan put on his trilby hat as Felina waved goodbye to us both.

"What did you do to change Miss Felina... magical fairy dust...?"

I laughed. "Actually, just listening, that is all."

Chapter Thirty-One

I needed a drink at the Jazz club with Tristan. I had earned better than I imagined, but I needed to steady myself before the thought of cooking for Edward and his lacklustre fiancée.

"I can't stay long, Tristan, just one drink. I have to cook dinner... and Edward... he's so picky...he'll tear me to pieces if I don't do everything to his <u>exacting</u> standards."

Tristan looked concerned.

"Jessie, you cannot go on like this, burning the midnight oil, being a slave to everyone... when is there time for Jessie... not Almodine and the issues she faces every day... Jessie?"

I couldn't answer that question. I could not imagine ever having money for a rent, never mind buying a house for Noah and I. Every time I went to church I thought of days that were chipping away... days, hours, weeks, without Noah.

Working for Bridget was my escape, it gave me a chance to walk away one day from Golda and Edward.

"You need to be aware of something, Jessie... An older gentleman, smartly dressed, formal... offered me a cigar... and money for the whereabouts of Jessie Lindemann. I didn't say anything of course. I am an old man. I have a bad memory. You need to be clever, keep your wits about you..."

"Who do you think it was... looking for me...?"

I felt worried, confused and shaken.

"Look... I told you... not to frighten you, but to be on your guard. You are on your way to a better life... you're young, but you are ambitious. You cannot let anyone stand in your way. You need to keep moving forward. No-one lives life looking in the rear view mirror. You are a good mother, and don't let anyone let you think otherwise."

"Tristan, I'm a lousy mother... I am ripping the days out of my diary until they formally decide I am an unfit mother."

"This is silly talk... let's get you a drink."

"I should get going, start preparing dinner... I should go..."

"Jessie, settle yourself down... besides maybe I need the company."

I drank my first drink quickly... double peach schnapps and lemonade. Tristan quickly bought me a second, followed by rum, followed by several fruity cocktails that had umbrellas and berries perched on lime and raspberry liquid. I had no idea what time it was, and besides I didn't care.

"The music is great in here tonight... that singer is great... reminds me of back in the day... you know, I was king of the pack with my polished shoes and slicked back hair. They called me the "Panther". I have no idea... the jet black hair and piercing eyes. I got attention."

I could feel myself letting go of any inhibitions.

"You still are the Panther! Shall we dance... let's go..."

Tristan laughed hysterically. "I haven't danced in forty years! I don't know if my knees would stand it!"

"Let's find out... Jessie and the Panther... it sounds like a song..."

Tristan was dancing like an animated young man, waving his arms around, and wailing with delight as I circled around him on the dance floor. We both felt free...

As I made my way back to my table, an olive skinned, dark haired young man gazed at me and smiled. His eyes were a fierce emerald green and I knew he was going to walk towards me.

"Who is the guy on the dance floor... your Granddad?"

I laughed, and I couldn't remember laughing in a long time.

"He is my good friend, my confidante... and younger than you and I..."

"I'm Xavier, can I get you a drink, and perhaps one for your friend...?"

"Thank you... two glasses of rum... would be great..."

"A rum drinker... mischievous, playful and exotic..."

"Well I am <u>none</u> of those things, so maybe you shouldn't buy the rum..."

"I haven't seen you around here... are you on holiday...?"

"Look, Xavier, I am not into small talk so you are wasting your time..."

Xavier was wearing a well-cut tailored jacket, and I didn't like the way he was looking at me. It was too intense. I wanted to leave, but I had no idea what time it was.

Tristan quickly interrupted:

"Shall I walk you home, Jessie...? It's not long until closing time..."

I couldn't quite take it in... how could it be closing time... wasn't I supposed to be buying food for Edward's dinner.

I couldn't remember, besides I didn't really care. The room was a blur. Xavier steadied me as I almost fell.

"She has had far too much to drink... will I go with her in a cab?"

"Tristan shook his head. "Xavier, I should have realised she couldn't hold her drink. I will take her home... get the cab."

"I'll take care of her..."

"Xavier, I know you can be trusted... make sure she gets home safely... she has been through a lot..."

"Of course... you look great Tristan, really well..."

"How's your music, Xavier, still composing? I remember your grandfather... a talented musician..."

"You know how it is... I write a lot... and sometimes I win... sometimes I don't. I am looking for a new piano... I had to sell the previous one... if you hear of anything, let me know."

"Of course... I will ask around... always old pianos in basements. I better write Jessie's address down on a piece of paper... oh and check she actually gets in the door safely will you Xavier."

"I will... you know I will... see you soon, Tristan."

Xavier and Tristan gave each other a hug, and I felt very sick.

The cab journey was a blur. I felt exhausted and leaned into Xavier's shoulders. I had no inhibitions.

"Wow, you have landed on your feet... this is like millionaire's row, isn't it?"

The imposing Victorian terrace now darkened at night looked less grand against the skyline.

"I hate the place..."

"Xavier's voice was soothing. "You are a bit of a mis-fit like me..."

Xavier was obviously very aware that I needed assistance walking up the steep steps to the front door.

"Jessie, be careful... steady yourself... another three steps..."

I tried in vain twice to attempt to open the front door with my key at an angle.

Xavier stepped forward: "Jessie, take a deep breath now... let me help... you will need a strong coffee..."

Xavier eventually opened the front door, and as I tiptoed gently through the austere vestibule Edward stood in my pathway, expressionless.

"What time do you call this, eh?"

Xavier stepped forward in an attempt to mask my inability to stand.

"Jessie has been a... little bit unwell... and I've been looking after her..."

Edward looked enraged: "What are you... her pimp?"

Xavier looked shocked: "I'm a musician, composer..."

Edward took control.

"Spare me your curriculum vitae... this failure standing here is <u>supposed</u> to be my employee, cooking dinner... and instead all I can smell from her is a brewery. She belongs in a sewer that one..."

Xavier held on to my arm as I felt I was going to fall.

"Look sir, I know you employ Jessie but I understand she has been through a difficult time..."

"Been through difficulties, living here... in grandeur. Breakfast, dinner and roof over her head in return for some light cleaning duties or cooking... that she has failed to do... I'll take the girl now... you can go home to wherever you came from."

"I promised Tristan that I would see Jessie was safe... I'm not sure I've done that if I leave her now. I will see that Jessie is safe with me until morning..."

I could feel Edward grab my arm, but it felt like candyfloss... I felt unable to make any clarity of the scenario that was unfolding before my eyes.

Xavier yelled: "Stop mauling the girl... she is not your property."

Edward was enraged: "A two-bit loser musician telling me what to do is not going to happen... get out of <u>my</u> property before I have you removed. Your choice.

Xavier tugged on my arm with an almighty pull.

"I am getting you out of here <u>now</u>. You cannot stay here... I promised Tristan I would see you alright..."

There was venom in Edward's eyes as he spoke so quietly I struggled to hear.

"You walk away now, Jessie Lindemann, and your time here is <u>terminated,</u> do you understand...?"

The rest of the evening was all a terrible blur. I woke up on an uncomfortable sofa with springs that were jagged and dug into my back.

A multicoloured crochet blanket covered me, and nausea swamped me.

"Where am I? Where is this? Have I done something wrong?"

"I'm Xavier from the Jazz bar, a good friend of Tristan. You are safe here, don't worry. The good news is I only do decent coffee. I have travelled all over the world... and what is it that I craved? Decent, rich coffee that would make the world a more magical place..."

Xavier held out an oversized mug of steaming coffee in a pretty cornflower blue pottery mug that looked home-made.

I was still disorientated. "What time is it? I - I - should have been at Golda's and... oh no... I - I... was meant to be cooking dinner for Edward and his fiancée... it was supposed to be scallops... I forgot to get the scallops."

Xavier laughed a raucous kind of laugh that endeared me to him.

"The scallops are the least of your problems. Your friend, Edward, sacked you in an indirect way. He probably hasn't, but he threatened it..."

"Why am I here... in the apartment of a total stranger? I can smell bagels..."

"Well I live above a bagel shop... warm bagels in the morning... it's good here..."

There was an array of expensive looking guitars hanging on the walls in a crazy kind of pattern that looked like zigzags.

"I can leave now, and I am so sorry for putting you to any trouble... Can I use your bathroom, I need to freshen up before work? I'll need to collect my things from Golda's... later on..."

"The place you live in would be miles to walk from here. Take your time... and then you can walk to Bridget's place from here."

Xavier was being kind, and I didn't trust it.

"Look Xavier, I don't want to sleep with you. I know I look desperate but I'm not. I need to get sorted out... I need to leave."

"I don't want anything from you Jessie... just to be a friend maybe... I've known Bridget for years... you know, it's an eclectic kind of neighbourhood."

I got ready quickly, washed my face and wondered how I would cope without the extra cleaning money at Golda's.

Xavier seemed kind, genuine, yet I was no fool. I had to keep ahead of the game. I couldn't let him get to know me, not now, or ever. This weekend was about Noah, and I was nowhere near ready.

"I'll walk you to work Jessie, I need the air. We can grab a bagel... throw a dice in the air... and choose something different.

I am different. I write songs all day... most of them no record company wants to buy, but there have been three songs that got the right artist... and I got to buy this apartment. It's not much, but it's mine..."

I smiled. "I like the apartment. It's lovely. Good energy. I feel you write there. The first time you saw the apartment it was at an auction. It was an empty shell... a repossession... and you saw the colour in the broken floorboards."

"I write with my first acoustic guitar, a bit scratched, frayed around the edges, but it has soul. Guitars are like people. Loyal. Different aspirations. Does your son play the guitar, Jessie? I could teach him if you want... no charge... you know, friends..."

I snapped. I was tired, and I felt afraid.

"What bit do you not understand? I don't need <u>you</u> or anyone else. You are suffocating me. Nothing is <u>free</u>. You cannot buy me or my son."

Xavier looked shocked and saddened.

"I - I'm sorry you feel that way. I didn't mean to cause offence..."

"Like I say, Xavier, best to leave me alone. Find yourself a nice girl... no questions, no answers."

Chapter Thirty-Two

Tristan greeted Xavier and I with a stunned expression.

"Were you out all night Xavier... what on earth..."

Xavier looked awkward.

"I should be going... good to, eh, meet you Jessie... take care... and see you around... you know... I play next door in the band..."

Tristan could not hide his concern: "See you, Xavier... take care..."

He looked intensely at my shoes which had not been changed since the night before.

"Please tell me you did not sleep with him Jessie. Please.... you have enough going on..."

"You are not my father or grandfather Tristan. Just because he walks me to my work does not mean we actually slept together. Do you have to be so judgemental?"

Tristan shook his head. "I have been around long enough to see the way that young man looked at you... so save your shenanigans for Bridget..."

"I think I've been sacked from the cleaning job... it's all gone a bit... well... Xavier dragged me away from Edward. They were like two lions... and they both were trying to outsmart the other."

Tristan sighed: "Maybe Xavier did you a favour... that Edward and his fancy friends are trouble. Let's face it, he will calm down because he wants a cleaner, cook and punch bag for less than the daily rate. You will pick up more hours here... you don't need them..."

"Tristan, this is a couple of days before Noah is visiting Bridget's. I need to show ability to earn. I need to show stability."

"It will fall into place for you... don't over think.

Bridget hollered: "Jessie... hurry up please..."

Tristan handed me a huge parcel wrapped lovingly in brown paper.

"It's for Noah... I just wanted to see it's alright with you... you know that he would like it."

"Can I open it now, Tristan?"

He nodded.

I tore open the brown paper just like a child.

"Wow... it's amazing... a limited edition train set... oh, Tristan... Noah is going to love this... he loves trains... thank you so much. It's so thoughtful..."

Tristan's face lit up: "Oh, and I just wanted to say that I am free Saturday in case you need me. I could be there for moral support..."

"As much as I would love to say yes... I think this is something that I am going to have to face alone. Thank you for always being there for me, unconditionally."

"I figure you need a friend, Jessie. You look out for everyone else around you, but who looks after the carers?"

Bridget walked towards me, her heels clicking... "A letter arrived for you yesterday... it's probably confirming details for Noah's visit... I got the carpets cleaned by the way, Jessie. The house is sparkling..."

I opened the rectangular envelope that was stamped in a way that looked official. I could sense before I opened it that it was not good news.

As I read the letter I felt like even the air suffocated me.

"I've missed two Psychologist appointments... I don't understand... I gave Golda and Edward's address. I should have received these letters but I didn't... I would never have missed these. I hated going, but I knew it was all part of it..."

Bridget looked dismayed. "You will have to telephone the office on the letter... re-schedule..."

This was like a thunderbolt, just before Noah's visit.

"What am I going to do now? It looks like I am not coping... like I don't really care..."

Tristan stepped forward: "It's one of these things. I miss doctor appointments all the time... you know... my age... forgetful."

Bridget snapped: "Put the tea on Tristan... if you don't mind..."

"You cannot go back to Edward and Golda's... if they have hidden letters... you cannot trust them... this is your future. Collect your things and move in with me. This has to be about stability. It has to be..."

Tristan carried the tray with the best china cups of tea.

"It has to be good you have had this setback <u>now</u> rather than the weekend. It just means that the weekend will go great."

"Do you think they will think I am harming myself... you know that I am not co-operating, that I cannot cope with <u>reality</u>. You know that I can cope with big concepts but not reality.

They are going to assume that I would miss appointments with Noah, that I am unreliable. Do you really believe I can come back from all this?"

Bridget looked pensive.

"Right now you have absolutely no choice. It's about fighting for your boy and you are not alone. That is what's important. You were before, and now you have us... and together we are powerful."

Chapter Thirty-Three

Bridget insisted that I stay with her, and prepare my mind for Noah's visit. I was not at ease. I could not settle. I felt like I was in a wheel of a hamster cage.

Bridge had kindly prepared me a room. It was not austere like Golda and Edward's in the rafters of the attic room. It was fresh, painted in soft linen white. There were French doors that looked on to the most beautiful garden that I had ever seen. There were bonsai trees, bamboo and amazing squares of clear water. There were huge white and pebble grey concrete rectangular structures holding exciting, vibrant plants of lime and fuchsia.

It was beautiful to see, yet I suddenly felt more alone than ever.

There had been too much change... the move to Golda's, the sudden arrival of Edward, the attack in Matty's apartment... missing the kindness of Barb and the pressure of being "Almodine" who had to know all the answers.

I had to know all the answers. I was being paid handsomely by Bridget to know everything.

The pressure of change was bubbling inside of me so much that my jaw felt locked together, so much so that it hurt.

I always carried a spare pair of sharp scissors in case the need arose.

I had a pair of scissors in my jacket pocket, and one in my bag.

It was time I faced the mirror. It was always important to face mirror. I had to see everything. I had to see the pain, the hurt seep out of every pore.

I took the sharpest blade of the scissors, took a deep breath in... and as I cut the top of my arm I exhaled.

It was enough... I cut a few more zigzag strokes... it was not hurting yet so I kept going... quicker flicks of blade on my tired flesh.

I was cutting good now, really good. I could feel it. I felt elated, ecstatic. I felt the control I had craved for so long.

"Jessie... I thought you were wanting dinner... Jessie..." Bridget was screeching but I could not hear her. I had dropped the scissors on the thick pile cream carpet... and my blood made it's mark.

I stood frozen as Bridget became more agitated.

"Jessie... are you alright...Jessie?"

Bridget's sixth sense drew her to open the door to my room... and as she witnessed me staring in the mirror with blood marking my pain like a map of the world she screamed uncontrollably: "Jessie... do not move. We need to get you an ambulance. Stay nice and calm, lovely girl... I will call them now."

I turned around, calm and smiling with contentment. The cutting made it better... it anchored me.

"No ambulance... get me bandages... I need bandages..."

There were no tears from me. No panic. Nothing.

I am not sure how long it took for the ambulance to arrive, but Bridget was crying like a baby and there was nothing I could say.

Bridget did not go with me in the ambulance. I travelled alone, as always.

"Your name?"

"Jessie Lindemann."

"Your address?"

"No fixed address."

"Is there someone who we can contact for you?"

"No... no-one."

The questions were the same carousel as before. I knew all the answers to say.

The nurse this time had kind eyes. Her face looked troubled. Too many worry lines on her forehead.

"Do you have any family, Jessie?"

"Eh... yes... I have a little boy... Noah..."

The nurse smiled.

"This antiseptic may sting quite a bit... try and be brave. I'll have you bandaged in no time... and have you as good as new..."

I remained silent. The realisation that seeing Noah had disintegrated into tiny pieces with every cut, with all the jagged edges.

"Doctor will be seeing you Jessie... just for a little chat... don't be afraid..."

"Probably they think I'm a lunatic... or some grey wasteland girl of emptiness..."

The nurse looked anxious: "The doctor... will be very... professional... there to listen..."

"They are going to take me away from Noah now, aren't they... sign horrible papers, so I never get to see him ever.

No. I want to sign out of here. I need to leave now..."

"That won't be possible, Jessie, I'm afraid... just take a few breaths..."

I don't remember anything after that. I was lying in a hospital bed.

"You haven't touched your food, Jessie, that won't help, will it?"

The nurse was different. She had a scraggy neck, and false eyelashes, and a smell of tar and liquorice about her.

"Once you have seen the doctor again, we can discharge you, so it's your lucky day..."

There had been no visitors. There were never any visitors but that was fine. It made it easier not to talk. The numbness always took a few hours to subside.

I was ushered into the office of a sterile room. The drabness was palpable.

"Genevieve Schelling. I don't want you to feel any way uncomfortable. It is merely standard practice... just to ask a few questions. I also have my card in case you would need to talk to one of my team out of hours..."

"That won't be necessary. I am fine, thank you... eh... should I pay you directly for the bandages... and the cream... I can pay for that now..."

"Jessie... that won't be necessary... I see it has been quite a long while since we saw you last... which is good, Jessie. This is improvement... it really is... Tell me about your work schedule... have you been kept busy without Noah?"

"I... I thought I had done really well. I was up at six a.m. to clean... and cook breakfast... prepare meals for Golda... and make sure I get the shopping list for the week. I have to have all the cleaning done by nine a.m. It is then that I work... doing my... counselling..."

Genevieve looked shocked and dropped her pen.

"Counselling? Really?"

I paused: "Well... not exactly <u>formal</u> counselling like you understand it... more... like psychic counselling..."

"Wow. Like a Psychic, Medium, Clairvoyant... I went for a reading many years ago... it was very enlightening... not that I should talk about that now. It was very interesting... opened a lot of doors to a new way of thinking for me..."

I looked at Genevieve's face... and read her.

"Michael... you will hear from him again... he is headstrong. He misses you... he still has the ring... and the keys to number twelve.

Oh, and Daria... she will be fine..."

Genevieve smiled. "Oh, my goodness... Michael was my fiancée from years ago. I always loved him... You say he kept the ring...? Really?"

"Next to the tapestry Beattie made..."

Genevieve was laughing: "The small tapestry picture of the hens... that Beatrice made... how funny...!"

"Thank you so much for that Jessie... and actually, it is clear to me you are intelligent, articulate, and bright... and I am going to throw you a lifeline to see your son, Noah.

You see, Jessie, I figure <u>everyone</u> in life deserves a chance... and you have been given a set of cards that many would have fallen at the first hurdle... but you haven't. You have <u>tried</u> with all your heart for your boy... and for that I commend you... I hold you in high regard, Jessie Lindemann.

I have the power to grant that you see your son on Saturday. I fully believe it is in Noah's interests to see his mother. You are a good mother, Jessie... I can see that, and I am a good judge of character. Besides... I <u>know</u> it is the right thing..."

"Do you have any questions, anything that you wish to discuss, that I can help you with?"

I was confused.

"Why would you help me... and not judge me when I made the mistake... the cutting...?"

"Jessie... this was a high pressure situation... and you have been working incredibly hard. You had not been using any alcohol, nor any other substances, and that tells me that is spontaneously linked with fear... you trying to regain a semblance of order.

You have not <u>fallen</u>, Jessie... it was just a stumble... you have to get up again... and it is safe here... no-one will judge you or laugh at you.

This visit is important for you and Noah. He still loves his mother, Jessie. He has not forgotten you."

I shuffled in my seat... I was not used to being believed.

"How could I ever repay you for helping me...?"

"<u>Show</u> me I am right Jessie, and that is reward enough for me..."

Genevieve turned around my life that day by giving me a chance when I was far from the shore.

Good people may be harder to find sometimes, but they are still there.

Chapter Thirty-Four

I knew instinctively it would be time to leave Bridget's after the incident.

She would not trust me in her home, and from that moment on, would never look at me the same way. Barb had offered that I could stay with her cousin, Kristin, who was a live wire, but kind hearted.

Kristin worked at a Casino by night, but wanted to be a professional singer.

She greeted me at the door with her hair in rollers and a cigarette hanging from her mouth. Jazz piano music played in the background. Nothing in the apartment matched. It was eclectic... jungle print orange zebra curtains and curved, unusual looking chairs, very sixties in style.

"You must be the kid... eh... remind me of your name?"

"Eh... Jessie?"

"That's the one... Kristin... I would shake your hand but I have a conditioning mask in my hair... algae... anti-ageing... algae works wonders..."

"Look kid, I ain't gonna bother you. I don't judge no-one. I made enough mistakes all of my own... so you don't have to feel like you can't be yourself... I hope we can be friends..."

Kristin was a whirlwind of good energy. I could tell that she was a kindred spirit.

"I stayed in New York for years, then went on a cruise and, you know... did a bit of this and that... landed a job as a singer... you should see the things I saw, Jessie... it would curl your hair, honestly..."

"I imagine..."

"I'm doing some self-improvement... (on the scrap heap) who wants a diva with laughter lines and enough spanx to fuel a hot air balloon. I need to be on my game... and I intend to be...!"

Kristin was a heart on your sleeve kind of person, and her sunny disposition was exactly what I needed.

"So feel free to help yourself to anything in the kitchen cupboards... and Thursday I always get take-out... So we could get pizza or whatever you want. Oh, and my friend Carla pops around... usually on a Thursday. She is totally harmless but she does tend to go on about her favourite subject, herself!

I heard from Barb that you are like a real life Psychic... Medium... like, seriously, how cool is that?"

I got a pack of tarot cards from Carla as a present actually... I have never had them out of the box as I have absolutely no clue how to use them. I got a crystal ball, second-hand from a costume/fancy dress shop... in like a big cardboard box of things they did not know what to do with.

Somebody told me that it's powerful... but it just looks pretty. I just leave it sitting on the book case.

Sorry... have I been <u>talking</u> at you... I am not like this all the time... I thought you might just want to hear a little about me... I know I can be a bit too much at times..."

I could see Kristin was trying too hard... Barb had probably told her my story.

"Well... I think it's great here... the apartment... it feels really homely. I know it's only temporary because you have a spare room, but I truly appreciate it."

Kristin smiled. "It's absolutely fine. We all need a start. You're young... I have spaghetti sauce... shall I heat some for you...? I don't mind... I always cook enough for twelve people and it's only just me."

I wasn't hungry, but it seemed right to say yes.

"I hear you are seeing your son tomorrow. You must be excited..."

I realised Barb had told Kristin most of my story.

"I suppose I cannot believe it's here... you know, it seems like it has been a long journey..."

Kristin threw a huge amount of pasta in boiling water from a great height.

"Do you like Parmesan cheese? I love it. I put Parmesan on everything..."

"What's your son's name?"

I hesitated. I didn't like the thread of this conversation. It felt uncomfortable.

"His name is Noah..."

Kristin stopped stirring the pasta so flamboyantly.

"Wow... cute name... do you have a picture?"

Of course I had a picture, yet I didn't know Kristin enough to show her.

"Oh... I think it is in my bags at my last place..."

"Here's some garlic focaccia... you'll need all your strength for tomorrow. The spaghetti won't be long..."

I could tell Kristin was a good person. Her eyes were clear, her smile sincere.

"Eat... you don't need to be polite here... trust me... I eat all day..."

The garlic focaccia was delicious. It tasted home made.

"Do you want Noah to live with you again... like in the same apartment, or maybe live with family...?"

I did not want to talk in such detail with Kristin, so I tried to divert her questioning.

"The bread it's delicious. Lovely..."

"So you don't know what you want I'm guessing... you're young... lots of responsibilities on your shoulders... I cannot imagine... I lost a baby... a few years ago... I suppose it wasn't really even a friendship when I look back. It was all... an illusion. I lost the baby on the kitchen floor. I didn't tell anyone... I ... you know, when the doctor looked at me he knew... I needed a clean up.

I often wondered what could have been. I suppose it's only the way it's meant to be... I don't know. I <u>think</u> about things you see... look at the bigger picture. I don't blank things out.

Oh, that's the spaghetti boiling over... I'm busy chattering..."

I suddenly did not feel hungry.

I ate the spaghetti slowly, while Kristin chatted about her vinyl collection.

Images of Noah flashed through my head. I could see Noah throwing the anorak I bought him into a puddle. I could see him alone, looking out a window into darkness, where there was no moon shining.

Tomorrow was my day to prove myself. I didn't know if I had the strength.

Chapter Thirty-Five

It was difficult to sleep, thoughts whirling around in my head.

I thought it best to wash my hair early... it took a while to dry.

I was to go to Bridget's house at ten a.m. which was going to be awkward enough as I had not stepped foot over the house since the night I lost control.

Bridget suggested I wear navy as it is inoffensive, and would make me look more sophisticated, smarter... not that all of that really mattered.

How was I going to be judged today? If Noah looks ill at ease in any way eyebrows will be raised.

I was stepping into quicksand, and there was nothing I could do about it.

I was ready quickly and closed the door to Kristin's apartment quietly.

I thought an early morning walk to Bridget's would be what I needed.

My hands felt cold, clammy and again pictures of how Noah looked the last time I saw him flashed intermittently.

It seemed a good idea to walk past the church. The hill was steep, but I took my time so I could see the beautiful stained glass windows glimmer in the morning sun.

I was drawn to walk inside the church. It felt the place I could never have to justify myself ever.

The church door was ajar and I walked quietly to light a candle.

On my path, kneeling and looking strained, was the young Priest I had met. I nodded as an acknowledgement.

I walked forward to pick up two candles, one for me and one for Noah. As I did so I could not help but cry, not for me but for how it all had come to this.

Genevieve, the Psychologist, had thrown a lifeline, but I was drowning. Noah would have to make the choice. A boy barely old enough to tie his own shoe laces.

The candles were lit and it eased my mind.

The Priest walked forward: "Can I help you... I mean it can help to talk to someone you don't know well..."

The young Priest looked genuine. His eyes intense, almost pleading with me to talk.

"Father... what do you do when you don't know the answer of how things are supposed to be the way they are? How do you know when to walk away from something you cannot do anything more about?

"Can I get your name again... I know we spoke before..."

"Jessie..."

"What or who would you like to walk away from?"

"My son... Father. My son."

"I have no proper home for him, Father. I am fighting to get a home, but it's harder than I thought. I... I... keep trying..."

"How old is your son?"

"He is five years old, in foster care until I can provide a stable home. What do you think I am meant to do Father? Do you have an answer?"

"Jessie, as you will be aware I am a Priest, therefore I have no children except my parish. My parishioners.

I do know this. It is not about material things, Jessie. It's about what you give in your heart."

"I am planning to give him away Father. The thought won't stop in my head. I haven't told anyone. You are the first person I have told.

I don't want my son looking over his shoulder every day wondering where he is next going to live... who will take him in for a couple of days. I want him to have a roof over his head... you know... the same roof over his head without being frightened.

I have fallen short as a mother, Father. I sent Noah to school without lunch money. I said I'd forgotten it when the school phoned. Then I stopped answering the phone.

I have a visit today and then I will put my plan into action. I will initiate the adoption... regarding Noah... so it is not dragged out... and he doesn't know where he is. I won't be one of those people that leave letters about my story or nostalgia. Noah needs a fresh start. A blank canvas, without me, and the quicker the better. My gut is telling me, quicker is best..."

The Priest listened intently.

"You are tired Jessie. I understand. You cannot or should not make a hasty decision that you may deeply regret years later. You do understand that, don't you Jessie. This is the biggest decision of your life. You have to take your time."

"Father, I have had plenty of time to think... many hours to know what to do... it is finding the courage to do it... will you pray for me, Father... will you pray for me...".

"Let's say a prayer together..."

I had burdened that young Priest with a heavy weight that morning.

As I left the church my mind was clearer. Much clearer.

Chapter Thirty-Six

I walked to Bridget's determined to get through the day with no tears.

I would have to keep the mindset that Noah was no longer mine. That would be easier.

I had the carrier bag with the present from Tristan. It had to be good fortune, surely.

I had washed my hair and scrubbed my fingernails clean. Who wants to be judged badly by a Social Worker? I had to at least keep up appearances.

Wearing some navy was better than black, softer, less harsh for a mother.

Actually, what is a mother supposed to look like? Who judges? Maybe it was me who judged myself.

I arrived at Bridget's. I was ready. I would walk through the day with as little emotions as I could. I could do this... I knew I could.

I rang the doorbell at Bridget's. The doorstep was adorned with lavish baskets of flowers. It seemed that Bridget was determined to give a good impression.

"Jessie... come in love... It's all ready. I've got some bowls of crisps, snacks, pizza slices, crackers, soft cheese, nice teas, oh and juices for

Noah... oh, and I could make Noah a smoothie... those fancy Social Workers would be impressed if I made a smoothie."

I tried to calm Bridget. I had never seen her so highly strung.

"I am sure they won't be looking at the food, Bridget... I suppose they are more bothered at how me and Noah are..."

"Jessie... let me show you the garden... I've borrowed a slide and a trampoline... you know I thought it would be a good idea... what do you think?"

"Great idea, Bridget. I better get ready... take my coat off... I can't quite believe it's all happening..."

Just then the doorbell rang. Bridget flew around the kitchen in a panic.

"Jessie... are the kitchen surfaces clean enough? I've sprayed them countless times."

"Bridget I need to answer the door... need to answer now..."

My heart was thumping. I adjusted my hair away from my eyes. I felt my hands clenching tightly. I was afraid. I didn't know what I was going to think or feel when I saw my son. I felt like jelly. I didn't know what to do, or think, or feel.

I answered the door slowly. A lady who looked in her early fifties with grey, wavy hair and oversized thick rimmed spectacles wore a grey overcoat, lilac scarf and carried a brown briefcase. She clutched Noah's hand.

Noah was taller than I remembered, and his hair had been cut too short. He was wearing an anorak I had not bought him, and his shoes were new. I would not have bought Noah that style of shoe... it looked wrong.

Noah looked right through me, like he did not know me.

I was afraid to speak in case I wasn't supposed to. I didn't know what I was supposed to do. The Social Worker looked reassuringly at Noah.

"Here is mummy. Let's go inside... and maybe have a look at some books..."

I felt agitated, ill at ease. I wanted to pick Noah up and hold him close... I didn't know what I was meant to do.

The Social Worker smiled. "Jessie, I am Helen... nice to meet you..."

She shook hands with me, but her hands felt cold.

"Do you want to sit on the floor with Noah... Jessie? Talk to him?"

Who was this woman to tell me what to do, like I was stupid?

"It is mummy, Noah... I hope you have enjoyed your... little holiday. I bet it's been good fun. I have got you a few presents to open..."

Noah didn't take his anorak off, and looked right through me.

"Here you are Noah... open the presents..."

Bridget hovered around the sofa adjusting cushions nervously.

"Can I get anyone a cup of tea... Dundee cake... oh, Noah, maybe a juice or a nice smoothie?"

Noah shook his head. "Gwen says I am not allowed smoothies... they are bad for my teeth..."

Helen shook her head. "I've just had a cup of tea, thank you... and I'm not one for Dundee cake... thank you all the same..."

It felt awkward, desperately awkward.

Noah opened his first present... a t-shirt with a dragon on it breathing fire.

Noah picked it up, looked at the dragon and sat the t-shirt down beside him.

"Gwen doesn't like dragons..."

It was like Gwen was in the room with us... the foster carer extraordinaire. I felt like I hated her right now, and I shouldn't feel like that.

I had to think on my feet. What would Noah actually want to do? What would make him trust the second rate mother who had abandoned him?

"There's a trampoline outside Noah... will we take our shoes off and see who can jump? I know you love trampolines!"

Noah looked at me intensely. "What if I fall, mummy, what happens if I fall?"

I tried to hold back the tears.

"You won't fall Noah, you <u>won't</u>. I'll catch you... you know I'll catch you..."

Noah looked at me in the eyes... then looked at his feet. The trust had gone. He had no faith in me. I understood that, and I deserved it, big time.

I had foolishly thought that Noah might have run to me at the front door... and everything could have been forgotten.... The rain, Noah being taken away... the electricity going out... and the cutting... the cutting that made me look like the biggest risk in Noah's life.

Of course Noah would want Gwen, whoever she was. She was a woman who took him to school, and tied his shoelaces.

Though Gwen wasn't the biggest barrier in Noah hating me. I had done a good job of that all on my own.

I thought it would be best to admit defeat to the Social Worker, when Noah turned to me, "Yes... I like trampolines."

The Social 'Worker was scribbling something irrelevant on a page, and I took Noah by the hand to the garden. Bridget smiled at me, the biggest beaming smile of support. Noah's face lit up as he saw the trampoline in the beautiful sunny garden.

Before knew it, I was whispering to Noah, "One day we will have a big house like this... with a really big garden... just like this... I will pick you up in my shiny new car... and it will be great... so much fun... I'm sorry, Noah, for what I did to you. I'm sorry. I've missed you every day... every second, every minute of every day."

I squeezed Noah's hand tightly.

I'll always be your mummy who loves you, no matter what..."

"Not helpful, Jessie. Not helpful at all."

I ignored the blandness of the woman, and jumped with my arms in the air like a jellyfish to make Noah laugh out loud.

Noah shrieked with laughter... like the way we used to be. The trampoline was safe... better than sitting in a goldfish bowl in Bridget's house.

"We could go fishing one day Noah... like I promised. Remember... the things I used to tell you... when I get a house with a big garden. I will get that house Noah... then it will be so different. It will.."

"Can I wear the dragon t-shirt to school, mummy? Can you tell Gwen that I can wear it? Can I... stay with you now?"

I could not look at Noah in the eye. How could I tell Noah he could not live with me right now, and that I was... before I had seen him... planning to give him away for good?

"It will be <u>soon</u>, Noah..."

"When mummy? When will I get to live with you again... Gwen says we are not allowed pizza. She says I daydream, and I should stop looking out the window. Mummy, I just look out the window to watch for you coming to get me."

"Noah, I will see you every week now, until we get our house. I am your mummy, not Gwen, so keep mummy's things with you... beside you... and it will feel like I am there... just until we <u>are together</u>."

"Gwen took my toys. All of them. She said she would keep them in a safe place but I don't know where they are."

I didn't want to hear any more about Gwen. I could sense that she had made a judgement about me. The <u>wrong</u> judgement, and she was trying to destroy my son. This was not what I had planned.

I was going to need the best lawyer money could buy, and that was going to cost money. I would have to earn it fast.

Spending the day with Noah was a whirlwind. I felt happy again, elated. Surprised at how happy I was to be a mother again. However, my opinion had drastically changed. Noah should be with me. It was best for him, and Gwen or any other bland, mindless Social Worker would rip Noah's heart out again, not while I was standing in front of him.

The Social Worker seemed to enjoy taking Noah by the hand... away from me. It gave her a false sense of power.

She probably had three children at home who never answered her back. Not ever.

"Put your coat on now, Noah. It's raining..."

Noah looked at me. I tried to smile reassuringly. I whispered:

"Soon Noah, soon."

Noah looked tired, pale. I want to run, push the Social Worker against the wall, and take Noah. We could run. We could run far away... down side streets where no-one could find us. Life isn't like than. It always catches up with you. Always.

You just keep moving forward, and never look over your shoulder. If you were to look back, you would get stuck in the labyrinth of the nostalgia. I knew that nostalgia was never transparent. It wasn't real. It's what we do when we want to fool ourselves that things used to be so great. Did they? Or were you a weaker person then?

Chapter Thirty-Seven

It was with a heavy heart that I knocked on Kristin's apartment door.

It was not that Kristin wasn't kind (she was).It's that she was intense, in an emotional sense, and with doing "readings" all day... trying to be Kristin's friend did not seem ideal right now.

Kristin was waiting on me. "Barb said you like pancakes... I have maple syrup, jam, chocolate... you name it..."

I was not hungry, but Kristin looked so animated and excited to see me.

"Once we have had the pancakes, we could watch an old movie, and then you can tell me all about Noah. Did it go well with Noah? Maple syrup on your pancakes?"

I did <u>not</u> want to eat, and I did <u>not</u> want to talk about Noah, but this was a place to stay. I would have to act interested.

"Thanks for asking... it was good... yes... it went well... I think..."

Eating the pancakes was like a haze. I realised I had been torn away from Noah, partly due to my failures, partly due to circumstance.

I ate the smallest amount of pancakes slowly... not savouring every bite. I had to meet with Genevieve the Psychologist again to talk about the visit, and how I felt about Noah.

Genevieve was like Barb. I was intuitive, and I knew I could trust her, and there were not many people I could trust.

If your child does not live with you, then people assume you are a monster. They assume you must be black of heart.

People can keep their assumptions. What do they know? Most people want categories, so you can fit in to what they expect of themselves.

Kristin talked incessantly, without pausing for breath. I smiled intermittently, and wondered if Noah was thinking of me, as much as I was thinking of him.

I apologised to Kristin, but I needed to sleep (or at least pretend I was sleeping)?

As I walked to the room, Kristin yelled: "You have a visitor Jessie... he wouldn't give me his name..."

I wondered if it was a debt collector, but I would be surprised if they had traced me here.

I walked reluctantly to the door. I was ready to explain myself, and I knew what to say.

The front door was ajar, but not open. I peered around the door tentatively. To my shock it was Edward, dressed in a black trilby hat, and soaked raincoat. He looked drawn, and bedraggled.

"Sorry to both you... I - I..."

I was shocked. How on earth had Edward found me.

"I didn't mean to startle you Jessie... I didn't know where to turn... my mother... Golda... she took ill last week... she had a fall... I... I wanted to contact you... she was asking for you... I didn't know what to say..."

Edward looked lost, and I felt compelled to ask him to have a cup to tea. "I don't want to impose, Jessie... I... didn't know what to do..."

"I'll get you a cup of tea Edward, and you can tell me what's been going on..."

"You know Fleur, my fiancée, she is in the south of France... she is pretty stressed... she needed time out... she could not deal with mother..."

"I imagine..."

"The thing is, I have work, and business meetings, and cannot be with mother... and deal with the tantrums... I was wondering..."

Edward took out his wallet, and took out a handful of notes and placed them on the kitchen table.

"I am sure this would help your situation..."

"So, let me get this straight, you got a Private Investigator, a good friend of yours, to trace me... to then offer me a cheap pile of cash to deal with your mother, is that right?"

"That makes it sound <u>contrived</u>, and rather <u>cheap</u>, Jessie."

"That's because <u>it is</u> cheap Edward. You cannot stand me. You never wanted me in your home. You treated me like dirt underneath your feet..."

Edward took out his wallet again, and put more notes on the table.

"Count it... it's real..."

At that point Kristin intervened. "I don't know who you are... but you look like a gangster in that hat, and my friend Jessie, is not for sale, so get out of here... you are not welcome..."

Edward looked at me downcast. I could sense he was desperate, and I also knew his fancy friends were nowhere to be seen.

"Triple the amount, and I will talk to your mother. I won't work for you, but I will talk to her... understand?"

"Could you talk to my mother now... she is not in great spirits..."

Kristin looked horrified. "Are you going to give in to that bully...?"

I walked to my room, and grabbed my small bag of clothes.

I picked up the money from the table, and stuffed it into my pocket. "I'm ready, Edward, let's go..."

"Kristin, I have to go... Golda needs me... and Edward does too... I <u>have</u> to..."

As Edward and I walked down the apartment stairs into the torrential rain his driver opened the door for me:

"I didn't think you would help me Jessie... I really didn't..."

"It's not for me... it's for my son. It's all for my son... it always has been, and always will be..."

Chapter Thirty-Eight

We arrived at Golda's and I was surprised. I felt numb. I was indifferent. I thought of the cash lining my pocket that was like a feather down quilt, and it made me feel good.

Edward thanked the driver (which was most unlike him) and smiled at me in an awkward manner.

"My mother may not be in a very good state... she has been having tests for her liver, her kidneys, her circulation, and her eyes..."

I sighed. It was always a joy to listen to Edward. He took pride in pessimism.

"Mother may be a bit out of sorts..."

'Out of sorts' was code for drunk... Edward walked in front of me (almost trying to shield me). Golda was slumped in the leather armchair in the drawing room.

"Edward you are hopeless, do you hear? What do you do for me? Nothing... you abandon me. You have always abandoned me..."

Now I could see why Edward was desperate to get me here. He could not cope with Golda. Working with Bridget and doing the readings had made me resilient.

Perhaps too resilient, and hardened of heart. I had heard it all. It was not all crystal ball, and prettiness.

"What's she doing here, Edward? She ran for the hills when the going got tough. She runs away from everything that girl. No use to anyone. Cat got your tongue girl... walk towards me... you are thinner than I remember you... a face like a weasel, eyes like a thief."

"Mother, please... Jessie has just arrived... she is our guest."

"You paid her Edward, handsomely I am sure... a thief she is...

I have dropped my spectacles... can you pick them up...?"

I leaned forward to try to reach the floor, but as I did so... Golda grabbed my shoulder towards her, and slapped my face. I was shocked. It stung, but didn't hurt. It was Golda at her very worst... brandy breath and aggressive.

"You, girl, are trouble. Take her away from here Edward..."

Typically Edward ignored the fact that his mother was like a wild animal... ready to lash out.

"Mother, please... just apologise... you wanted Jessie..."

"Take the girl away from here... She stole money from my handbag. She stole my eternity ring. Are you going to allow this thief and runaway into our house again? Once we were fools... twice we were stupid."

201

"I didn't steal anything... not money... not a ring... nothing..."

"I've got a surprise for you Jessie, a real surprise that you will appreciate..."

"What is it, Edward?"

"Oh, trust me Jessie Lindemann... it's everything you truly deserve..."

Chapter Thirty-Nine

The doorbell rang, and Edward calmly walked to the door. I wondered if it was his fiancée, or maybe carers for Golda. I was confused.

A policeman accompanied by a blonde haired policewoman with solemn expression nodded at Edward.

"Jessie Lindemann... you don't have to say anything..."

I was in shock. It was all a bad dream. I had the cash Edward had paid me which I thought was in relation to caring for Golda.

I had been set up. It was pieces of a jigsaw all fitting into place.

Edward was no victim, neither was Golda. She was a wealthy alcoholic, wallowing in the past. Edward, a spoiled boy with no integrity.

I said nothing, looking straight ahead. I had no idea how I was going to get out of this.

Edward looked shocked as my arms were placed behind my back, and the policewoman explained I would be handcuffed. Edward tried to intervene:

"Surely Jessie does not need handcuffed. I mean... it's not as if she is a danger..."

"We will decide sir, what kind of threat she poses to the public..."

Edward looked shocked. "I thought she was just going to get a warning. I - I - didn't think..."

"Sir, we will take her to the station... thank you for locating her..."

I was led away firmly, while Edward looked horrified.

The rest was all a blur. Being in the back of a dark police van when I was completely innocent was bewildering.

I didn't make a fuss. I just sat quietly. There was no point in making things any worse. I was aware things looked bleaker than ever for me and Noah.

In fact, let's not use the word bleak, more like impossible. Gwen, foster carer extraordinaire, would not see me as a criminal.

How could I talk to the Psychologist after this? She would be afraid of sitting in a room with me in case I attacked her.

The doors of opportunity for a new life seemed to be closing. However, sometimes in life fate intervenes... and, against the odds, things can turn in your favour.

It seemed while I was sitting alone in the back of the van that had a foul smell of faeces... Kristen had telephoned Barb. Kristen had felt something was wrong, and she always trusted her gut instinct.

When Edward had offered me the money to visit his mother, Kristen was not only a witness, but had picked up a diamond ring... (which she assumed was mine). She held the ring for safekeeping, but Barb had telephoned the police, concerned for my welfare, especially as I had just had my supervised visit with Noah.

I was taken to a small room in the police station, and made to wait. I was told nothing. It seemed like hours. There were bricks to count, and a wasp to stare at that flew too close to my eyes.

The same policewoman who seemed to delight in my fear, brought in her sidekick.

"We are just gathering additional evidence Miss Lindemann. Is Jessie the name on your birth certificate?"

"No, it's Jessica, but I don't like Jessica. It's just plain Jessie..."

"I see... got a lot of strong opinions, haven't we Jessie Lindemann and, from our experience, strong opinions get us into trouble."

"I haven't done anything wrong. I'm innocent..."

"How did you manage to have three thousand pounds cash in your handbag... that did not happen to be in your bank account previously?"

"I was paid..."

The policeman sneered. "Are you a prostitute, and if so, how many hours of work is that for... you must be pretty good, love..."

"I'm not a prostitute..."

"Who is your pimp, love?... and was Edward your former client who got angry because you got a boyfriend?"

"Like I say, I am no prostitute..."

"Don't play with us, Jessie, that's not pocket money... and that sum of money went missing from Golda's safe.

You had access to that safe. You were a cleaner. You worked there... you preyed on an elderly lady from a wealthy background, and befriended her for your own gain. A con-woman who consistently stole from a woman who had given a roof over your head. You betrayed her trust, didn't you?

You think that because you have cut yourself like a butcher we will let you walk away from here...? Think again young lady.

You are cold, calculating, a liar, and a thief, and no half-baked Psychologist will get you off the hook either..."

"I am innocent. I want to see a lawyer."

"She is quite the little madam this one, demanding a lawyer, and opinionated...

You can sleep in a cell overnight and see if that knocks some sense into you..."

The cell was dank, and had a smell of urine, and a distant smell of cooked meat pie that had seen better days. This was thinking time, yet I had to find a way out, and fast.

Surely Barb would know a really good lawyer... a former client who wanted to do a good turn. Barb was well-loved, and right now I needed her more than ever.

Chapter Forty

Barb, one of my dearest friends and confidante, arrived at the police station dressed in sharp charcoal grey pinstripe suit, nude heels and matching grey clutch bag.

"I want to see Ritchie. Ritchie Kennedy."

The police officer looked bemused.

"Let me rephrase that. I have the lawyer, Oliver Cairnmure Wood, with me... Ritchie will be expecting me..."

The policeman looked anxious: " I have head of Mr Wood... but doesn't he represent high profile clients...?"

"I'll pretend I didn't hear that young man... I am high profile..."

"Eh... please take a seat in the waiting area..."

Barb took out her mirror from her handbag, and touched up her nude lipstick...

Barb always had to be the centre of attention. She looked over her right and left shoulder and scanned the people sitting opposite her in the waiting area.

Barb was a people watcher. She always told me: "I can see what someone earns per year, not by their shoes, but by their face..."

I thought, surely it was their shoes, but Barb was insistent. "A face shows everything, every line, a sun-dial to the soul."

I always remembered that.

Ritchie Kennedy, a tall confident looking detective with a swagger, stopped suddenly and looked anxious at seeing Barb.

Ritchie walked over the Barb (trying to appear calm). "What the hell are you doing here... one of your pimp boyfriends been taken in or what?"

"Don't be smart with me Ritchie, what with a naughty newspaper scandal that could come your way if you're not careful... you'll be the one needing the pimp, not me..."

"Full of banter as usual Barb... and looking very nice... if you don't mind me saying... (with or without the Botox).

"Cut it Ritchie... I need a favour... el pronto... and if you can do this for me... I'll throw in Libby and Cat, your favourite girls, as my little thank you. I know how you like your threesomes, Ritchie boy... or is it all in the past now? Does your wife dress up for you now?"

"Shut it, Barb. Do you want to use a megaphone while you're at it?"

"A friend of mine: young girl... Jessie Lindemann... going through a bad time. She's got a little boy... struggling... decent kid... no family... give her a break will you."

"Give me the name again... and she'll be released by tonight... no charge..."

"What, you don't need me to call Oliver...?"

"Not necessary, Barb. Like I say... she will be released without charge... and shall I let you into a secret? I _love_ when you ask me to do things for you... it keeps it real... you know what I'm saying...

Oh, and I like the new girl... not got much to say but you know a commercial asset when you see it. I like that..."

"Ritchie, cut the dirty talk and see to Jessie... I want any evidence destroyed, and no trace of her being detained. She has to get her boy back.

Everything erased from files... you got it..."

"It's under control Barb. Can I get you a coffee..."

"More like a gin and tonic and a fumble with you Ritchie boy..."

"I'll go sort things out..."

"Friends forever, Ritchie boy... friends forever..."

Chapter Forty-One

I heard a knock on the cell door.

"Jessie Lindemann... you are free to go... It seems there has been a mistaken identity..."

I knew I had to be truthful: "No. I'm Jessie Lindemann. I do... I mean I did work for Edward and Golda. I mean, I did speak to Edward..."

"Look, kid, I don't need your life story. Just beat it. Let me give you your things and you are free to go, as in free... there will be no charges."

I couldn't believe it. "Is this a dream? Do I have to be in a cell longer?"

"Beat it kid, before I change my mind. Oh, and there will be no record of you being here... I understand you are fighting for your son..."

It was confusion, mixed with elation.

"What about the three thousand pounds in my bag that Edward gave me to see Golda. I'm a cleaner, you see..."

"Look kid, call it your lucky day. Maybe you should say thanks to a good friend of yours... She is a firecracker that one..."

"Barb?"

"Oh, and if you stick with Barb you'll do OK in life... you could do a lot worse."

"Thank you for everything... you'll never know how much I appreciate what you've done..."

"Stay away from that Edward... he's rotten through and through that one... you had a lucky escape... Life is full of second chances... (I've had plenty of my own). Oh, and good luck with your boy..."

I had no idea who the detective was, and I was not going to ask Barb any questions. Barb was waiting for me, looking surprisingly calm.

"You can stay with me... I don't need that Bridget interfering..."

" I was supposed to have been at work... She made it clear, I was on a warning..."

"Forget Bridget. She does alright, taking the huge cut from every reading you do, while she sets out the crystal ball on the coffee table. She looks after herself that one..."

"She gave me a chance though, Barb."

"You've lined her pockets, and don't you forget it."

Barb could never see a differing point of view. It was her way or the highway.

"Anyway, like I say... you can stay at mine... and I don't think that Edward will be bothering you again... that's for certain sure..."

I knew he wouldn't, not in a million years...

Chapter Forty-Two

Barb made me a hot chocolate with so many marshmallows and toffee pieces, the chocolate was spilling from the glass.

Barb, it had to be said, was not the 'motherly type'.

"What happened today with posh boy Edward, that is a warning for you... do you understand?"

I was confused. Barb was going to give me a long winded story...

"Warning, as in keep your wits about you... trust no-one."

"But does that not mean then you are always looking over your shoulder if you don't trust?"

"No it doesn't, Jessie. It means you are protecting yourself. You <u>never</u> want to be thrown in a cell again... <u>never</u>."

"Barb, I know this. I was naive, but I am not stupid..."

"You were set up by a man with a personality of a rattle snake... you need to learn from it..."

"What, don't walk on the grass?"

"You need to get out of here... it holds too many bad memories for you. Life has all been about a game of snakes and ladders, and you sliding down ladders, and back to square one. This needs to change. I'm the only family you've got. Me and Noah are all you have..."

"I've got Bridget... Tristan..."

"Look love... Bridget has been bankrupt so many times she has had to sell her coat hangers... She is what she is... exploits the vulnerable, the needy, the helpless."

"Are you saying Psychics aren't real? Are you saying I acted fake... telling lies?"

"Jessie, you are making enough money to eat. Not much else. Bridget doesn't see herself short... always been the same... at least I treat my girls with respect and dignity."

"Barb, you girls are prostitutes... whores... Bridget hires Psychics..."

Barb looked at me blankly: "Psychics, prostitutes, what's the difference?"

I was speechless. I really could not think what to say.

"Jessie... Prostitutes are not whores. They are simply doing what you do - a service. Like it or not, there is no difference between the two occupations.

I just keep it real, Jessie. I have <u>seen</u> it all, <u>heard</u> it all, but I'm no whore, neither are my girls. They are mothers, daughters, sisters, with bills to pay, and children to feed.

Have I exploited my girls? No. I pay the highest rate, and what do I get in return? Loyalty, that's what... and I tell you... that's rarer and rarer these days. You cannot put a price on loyalty.

I've had to watch my back all these years, 'course I have... So when I warn you to get out of here, it's because <u>I care</u>."

"What about that I'm working for Bridget. I'm helping people... change their lives?"

"For pennies Is this what you want for Noah... <u>scraping by</u>? Is it?"

"Barb, I know what you are trying to do. You are twisting things so I doubt myself and think I have to give away Noah to Gwen or some other rancid woman who has the personality of a battery.

I can tolerate Gwen because she is a foster carer. She is temporary. I don't want to give away Noah to someone else <u>forever</u>. It's too long, and it's not fair..."

"Jessie, I am not asking you to give away Noah. Far from it. I want you to fight, but to fight you'll have to get out of here... go to the countryside... where there is less noise, less people and less judgement.

Show Noah the world, where he can go, what he can achieve.

Give him a compass, an adventure. A life."

"Could Noah and I stay with you...?"

Barb paused, and gave me a steely stare. "No, you can't. You cannot handle what I do, and Noah should be as far away from here as you can run."

"But you are not a prostitute, Barb, you just organise everything, like a manager."

"Don't kid yourself. Why can I run this global operation, girls in every country? Well? You tell me. I'm one of those girls well... <u>was</u> one of those girls. I lay on my back for money, hard, cold cash. It wasn't pretty. It wasn't kind, but it gave me a photographic memory.

I have been where you are. The bed and breakfasts, the hostels, and under a railway bridge.

Take Noah away from this."

"Barb I may lose Noah, when we go to Court..."

"I have a good lawyer, or should I say, a team to get me out of any situation, if you know what I mean. I don't need to be a Psychic to tell you that you have to move away..."

"The hot chocolate was lovely, Barb, thank you..."

"My personal chef got me the chocolate... pure indulgence..."

"You must be proud of yourself, Barb, a personal chef, apartments, cars, house boat..."

"They are all <u>things</u> Jessie. I went out to get as much money as I could, and in doing so I actually forgot about myself.

Don't do the same as me, Jessie. You have the power to change it all for you and Noah.

But only you can decide..."

Chapter Forty-Three

In a whirlwind of time, I had to face Bridget again. I would have to explain why I had not turned up Wednesday, Thursday and Friday.

Instead of me being greeted by Tristan, my trusted friend, a young woman adorned in oversized gold chains, jet black long wavy hair and a checked skirt and scarlet top three sizes too small for her.

"We are not open yet, love. I can take your name for an appointment later on with one of our trusted Psychics (exceptional in their field)."

Unfortunately the fact that the young woman chewing gum and reading a script from a card looked decidedly unprofessional.

"Sorry, there must be some mistake... I work here."

"Do ya? Really?"

The girl looked me up and down while still chewing her gum.

"You must be Almodine, the unreliable Psychic... that's why Bridget phoned my cousin. I'm getting double time seeing it's short notice...

The name is Shimmer because my mum says I light up a room.... like a chandelier..."

It was apparent to me that 'Shimmer' was a terrible stage name for a Psychic, and this girl was a fake. Real Psychics can tell real Psychics... that's how it works.

"Where's Tristan?"

Oh.... the <u>old guy</u>. He collapsed so he is not well at all..."

"What's wrong with him?" I couldn't believe what I was hearing. Tristan seemed invincible. I wondered if Xavier, the musician, had his address. I couldn't really speak to Bridget.

As I thought of her, Bridget appeared.

"In my office please Jessie."

'Shimmer' could not hide her contempt for me. "Shall I make a coffee for you Bridget, and maybe do some dusting and hoovering? Nothing is too much trouble for me. I know you've been let down in the past."

Bridget ignored Shimmer. Her face like thunder.

"Take a seat. Noah's Social Worker has been trying to arrange to speak to you about a visit with Noah. You were unreachable on the phone. You are completely off the radar most of the time. As a mother, as an employee, you are falling short of the mark."

After questioning and time in a police cell I did <u>not</u> need a speech on working hard from Bridget.

I could phone the Social Worker, but not in front of Bridget. I needed some privacy. I needed to see Tristan's smiling face, to feel he understood me.

"You have left me no choice. Your hours are cut. You can work two days a week. Shimmer and two new part-time Psychics will take over your hours."

I could not take it all in. I felt Bridget was turning her back on me without knowing the facts.

"Please, Bridget, I can explain... please..."

Jessie, I have been down this road countless times with you, and now I have to think of the business... As you are aware, I have built my Psychic brand from nothing.

I will not allow you, or anyone else to jeopardise my name. Do you understand that?

I had detectives here asking questions about you, and I am going to make it easy for you... If I find out you are involved in anything I don't like, you are out, no questions asked."

"But Bridget, I was set up. I was wrongly accused."

"Jessie, I am afraid I don't want to hear it. You can have two days, because the regular clients seem to like you. Take it or leave it."

"Why am I on basic wage, when Shimmer waltzes in the door on double time? I'll never get a place for Noah and I on basic."

"You are pushing me, Jessie. I've been good to you when you cut yourself and we had to cover it up. I had no previous addresses for you. I had no references, but I gave you a chance. Not many would have.

You were lucky, and you blew it. Do you hear? You blew it. No-one to blame but you, and your own son pays for it every single day. Every day, Jessie. Think of Noah, and not yourself for once.

Oh, and there are the details for Tristan if you can drag yourself to see him."

That was the point I realised Bridget had washed her hands of me. I had to be realistic.

Shimmer belonged to a fairground, and couldn't 'read' anyone for toffee.

"I'll stick it Bridget, thanks very much. I've been good to you too, reading for clients no-one else wanted. I worked night and day for you, and you took fifty per cent of my earnings.

When would I ever get a flat? Never, that's when... trapped. You pretend to be so caring when you use Tristan, and pay him a pittance also... As long as you have your holidays all over the world where I paid for it. I was so exhausted with all the readings, while you crammed in clients back to back for your pocket.

There are clients who pay a fortune for readings to know about a rosy future they won't have. You don't stop them over-spending for advice they can ill afford. You take it like a <u>vulture</u>, over and over until you bleed people dry. I will gladly leave Bridget.

Thank you for exploiting me, when I had no other choices..."

Bridget was in shock. I had been in a torrent of rage at Bridget accusing me of not thinking about Noah. Something in me had snapped, and it felt good. It felt like a weight had lifted off my shoulders. I suddenly felt free... like, strangely, I could do anything I wanted, anything at all.

I didn't look over my shoulder when I walked out, nor did I look at Shimmer. I would phone the Social Worker to see Noah, before I would decided what to do.

First I had to see Tristan. He believed in me and, despite it all, I would never let him down.

Tristan shone a light wherever he stood. He gave all the clients hope, and that's all anyone needs in reality. Hope.

Tristan was in hospital miles away, and on the way there I would hopefully see Xavier.

Tristan and Xavier were alike in energy, and I felt safe with that, as strange as that may sound.

Xavier understood my path very well as a musician. I could trust him, I needed that empathy right now.

Chapter Forty-Four

It felt right to try and find Xavier at the Jazz bar and let him know about Tristan.

I didn't feel comfortable going into the bar alone. I didn't want to give the wrong impression.

I couldn't believe it when Xavier was sitting hunched in a Merlot coloured velour booth in the corner. Candelabra shining above him, lighting up his kind eyes.

"Hey Jessie, great to see you. Let me get you a drink... I was just writing song lyrics. You know how it is... when you want to think up amazing lyrics, you can think of nothing and when you least expect it... everything comes to you..."

Xavier had wisdom beyond his years.

"Xavier... I am not here for a drink.... I am here about Tristan... I just heard he's been taken ill and in hospital. I need to see him..."

Xavier nodded: "I assumed you knew. No-one ever thinks of Tristan as an old man. He is a trailblazer. I suppose his age has caught up with him... he's a fighter, Jessie... I need a cigarette outside before we go to any hospital. I need to be relaxed when Tristan sees me... or he will panic..."

"I don't smoke, Xavier..."

"Look Jessie, you need to lighten up... live once in a while... walk outside with me... to the balcony..."

I didn't want any poetic conversations with Xavier. I was not getting a good feeling about Tristan and I didn't like the idea about him being alone. I wanted to let him know that Noah loved his train set. I wanted to tell him <u>everything</u>, like I always did.

"Cigarette, Jessie?"

"Why not, yes, I mean, no... I better not... I mean..."

Xavier smiles: "Just take a cigarette, and I'll give you a light.... now take in the view from the balcony... you can take in <u>everything</u> from here... literally everything... What do you see?"

I looked around, but drew a blank.

"I can see... people... lots and lots of people... it's a city... weaving in and out in all directions..."

Xavier looked at me intensely, with a neutral expression. "Where is everyone going?"

"Look Xavier. I do love our philosophical conversations, but Tristan is lying in a hospital bed, I am supposed to see a Psychologist to check I am not insane enough to look after Noah, and phone a Social Worker all in the space of one day."

"Forget that. What do you really see outside, right in front of you..."

"Xavier, honestly... I'm tired of this, I don't see anything. Nothing at all."

"<u>Jessie</u>, au contraire. Everything, all of humanity is on display here, and do you know the best thing of all?

<u>No-one</u>, not one of us, actually knows where we are going."

I had no idea what Xavier was really talking about, but I accepted maybe I was meant to hear the words.

Xavier always seemed to make me think of his swords, days after he spoke them, and that is rare.

I wanted to see Tristan, and I knew when I touched his hand that I would "see" things more clearly.

Social Workers could wait, it was Tristan that would tell me what to do. I knew I had to hear what he would say, he was like the family that were nowhere to be seen, and maybe I was family to him too. We were perhaps sent to each other, serendipity. Who knew...

Chapter Forty-Five

Xavier and I sat quietly in the cab to the hospital. Xavier was tense, and was fidgeting with a cigarette paper, folding it over and over like origami.

We arrived, and Xavier, unsurprisingly, announced that he needed another cigarette and he would meet me inside.

The lift smelled of a dank, musty smell of raincoats and strong cough lozenges.

Tristan was on level 3, and my whole body felt warm, then cold and normally I could "tune in" to what I would see, but not today.

I was ushered to the door of a private room, and I was confused by what it all meant.

"It's family only..." the nurse snarled abruptly.

Tristan had no family to speak of except Bridget, so I had to think on my feet.

"I'm his daughter..."

She looked at me up and down. "You are not on the form..."

"Step daughter... I've been out of the country for a while so dad thought it was easier... just to leave me off the form... you know how it is... we get older, and we forget things..."

The nurse pursed her lips: "I'll have to let Admin know about any changes... your father is extremely ill..."

Tristan shocked me. He suddenly looked more fragile than I had ever seen him... drawn, his skin sallow, and his eyelids charcoal grey.

There were lots of tubes leading who knows where, a labyrinth of wires that bleeped continuously.

I wanted to run out of the room and hide, but I couldn't.

I walked slowly to the hospital bed. Tristan's eyes were closed.

I gently pulled a chair next to his bed, and took his hand and placed it gently in mine.

"I'm sorry I wasn't here for you... there was a lot happening... Edward and Golda... I have walked away from all of that...

I wanted to let you know that Noah loved the train set. It all went fine, the visit, better than expected, thank goodness for the trampoline or I would have had to talk to the Social Worker about the temperature outside, and manure on the roses.

You told me to be on my best behaviour and I was. You would have been proud of me. I didn't mess up, and that is not like me, is it?

Open your eyes Tristan... just so you can see me... your hand feels nice and warm... that has to be a good sign, hasn't it? You are going to be getting your dancing shoes on soon, and getting out of here in no time... I have faith... oh, and Bridget has hired a fake called 'Shimmer' who just needs a broomstick. She has more 'props' on the table than a Broadway show... like, seriously. Just wait till you see her... I thought that would make you laugh. It didn't make me laugh, I was waiting on a comedian, and a magician to walk in next... and take the floor... you have to laugh don't you, Tristan? You told me that... you see, I have never told you properly... how you helped me... I mean, <u>really</u> helped me. It's not about throwing money at people, is it? It's about having 'time' for them, and you have always had time for me... Please open your eyes... or squeeze my hand, or laugh, or dance around the room like you used to... Just let me know that you can <u>hear</u> me. I know you won't leave me, it's not going to happen... you are going to get better...

They might be a bit miserable in here... but they will make you better... I just need you to know that I am <u>trying</u> to be a better person... like to do things <u>properly</u>. I'm trying to <u>change</u> Tristan... honestly... I am trying to be a <u>different me</u>."

"Visiting time is over, dear... you can see him tomorrow..."

"Will things go fine with Noah, Tristan? Will I know what to do? <u>Please</u>, please tell me that... Will you send me a sign on what I should do?"

At that moment, I felt a strong squeeze of the hand. A forceful squeeze of the hand.

"It's time to leave now, dear..."

"I need to say some more... I'm not ready..."

"Tomorrow dear... tomorrow."

I was led away by the nurse, and Xavier had waited sheepishly outside.

I peered in the glass window at Tristan, and refused to cry. Tristan had to see me smiling and waving.

Xavier put is hand on my shoulder, and said nothing at all.

We sat in the cab in silenced. I didn't want to hear anything at all and for once, neither did Xavier.

Chapter Forty-Six

Genevieve ushered me to her office. It wasn't like she was a 'real' Psychologist. It was as if she was more of a friend. Of course, that could be more of a façade, but I trusted her.

"Your visit with Noah went extremely well, Jessie... This is tremendous news and I understand Gwen noticed a real 'upturn' in Noah's behaviour. A vast improvement."

I felt heartened. Noah could obviously see through foster parent extraordinaire, Gwen, just like I could.

"Yes, Noah was a lot more stable in school too, so I propose to allow an 'unsupervised visit' next time for you and Noah. I understand you both need your 'freedom' and being watched by a Social Worker is less than ideal for you.

"Oh, I thought I would have to answer lots of questions today... I was prepared..."

"I am not here to test you Jessie. I am merely here to be a facilitator, to be part of your journey..."

"Do I have to fill in forms before the unsupervised visit, or afterwards..."

"Jessie, don't worry about any of that, the Social Worker will take care of the papers before Court..."

"Court?"

I didn't want to hear that word, Court, where everyone else would decide about me and Noah, a panel, or a Judge, faceless people who didn't know who I am...

"Do you think they will let me keep Noah? What do you think?"

Genevieve suddenly looked uncomfortable.

"I am not a family lawyer, Jessie. I do know they do try and keep mothers and children together... if at all possible... but sometimes other factors come into play..."

I couldn't believe what I was hearing. I thought Genevieve was 'on my side', my friend, a confidante... but she was the same as Gwen. Exactly the same. Wearing the copycat mask.

"I'm not sure a Judge would know that being a Psychic was a real job... you know tea leaves, head scarves, crystal ball. I mean, I am sure your Social Worker will go through the 'relevant' paperwork to prepare your case in the best way you can. What I would suggest is that your personal reference of Barbara who runs a prestigious Escort Agency (or brothel) may raise eyebrows."

Genevieve's mask had slipped.

"Thank you for your well meant advice... I'll bear it in mind."

I knew exactly what Genevieve was saying. I understood it loud and clear.

Chapter Forty-Seven

It was a Wednesday, and I wore the new navy coat Barb had bought me, and red shoes with my money from Bridget.

I was meeting Noah in a café, and I had planned to take Noah for new shoes.

Gwen brought Noah to me with a smug look on her face.

"I have written down that Noah's clothes were pristine when I dropped him off to you. It's always better to write too many notes for Social Services, than not enough I find. I've been doing this for years.

I have a no nonsense approach, no luxuries, no fripperies, and knowing where they stand.

Children, whatever age they are, like to know where they stand, I find..."

I smiled sweetly: "Yes, I do agree Gwen. I do truly hope to learn from you..."

"I do have many books on parenting. I charge for copies mind, but I am willing to provide you with lots of useful and helpful information."

"I will certainly take that on board... anyway, we are going to be shopping and having a late lunch so... will see you soon."

Gwen tried to smile, but instead it was a grimace.

" I shall see you later, and Noah's jacket is dry-clean only, so <u>be aware</u>."

"Oh, yes Gwen. I shall be aware."

Noah looked pleased to see me, and I felt my heart in my mouth.

"Wave to your Auntie Gwen, Noah. Wish her a lovely day... see you soon..."

Noah and I waved in the most animated way I could muster.

At that moment I could feel Tristan with me, mouthing the words, as if he were right in front of me:

"Today, Noah, we are going to play a game. It's called hide-and-seek, but a really magical version where mummy shows you how good she can hide, and hiding can be lots of fun."

Noah looked puzzled: "Where are we hiding, mummy?"

"First we have to run... like the egg and spoon race... we have to run fast until I say stop, which is even more fun, right?"

Noah laughed: "Yes, it is..."

"Run faster Noah, take my hand tight."

Tristan was running with me on my right side.

"Do you remember what Tristan bought you as a present? Well, look what is right in front of us now..."

"Are we going on a train now... today... I thought we were getting a sandwich..."

"Noah... where we are going we can build lots of sandwiches. Tristan opened the door for us on the train and sat right next to Noah.

"You see Noah, look out the window and don't be scared."

"But where are we going, mummy? Where?"

"Oh, that doesn't matter Noah, anywhere but here..."

Tristan smiled.

"You see, Noah, I maybe haven't given you lot of things so far, but today... I will give you the world..."

"But I can't see it mummy."

"But I can... Dear Noah, I give you the World..."

Printed in Great Britain
by Amazon